PLAY THE GAME

THE HOOP CON

PLAY THE GAME

GAME

THE HOOP CON

AMAR SHAH

SCHOLASTIC INC.

Copyright © 2024 by Amar Shah

All rights reserved. Published by Scholastic Inc., *Publishers since 1920*. SCHOLASTIC and associated logos are trademarks and/or registered trademarks of Scholastic Inc.

The publisher does not have any control over and does not assume any responsibility for author or third-party websites or their content.

No part of this publication may be reproduced, stored in a retrieval system, or transmitted in any form or by any means, electronic, mechanical, photocopying, recording, or otherwise, without written permission of the publisher. For information regarding permission, write to Scholastic Inc., Attention: Permissions Department, 557 Broadway, New York, NY 10012.

This book is a work of fiction. Names, characters, places, and incidents are either the product of the author's imagination or are used fictitiously, and any resemblance to actual persons, living or dead, business establishments, events, or locales is entirely coincidental.

ISBN 978-1-338-84031-5

10 9 8 7 6 5 4 3 2   24 25 26 27 28

Printed in the U.S.A.   40

First printing 2024

Book design by Stephanie Yang

**ONCE AGAIN,
TO TEJAL, ROHAN, AND ANNIKA**

TABLE OF CONTENTS

SPICE BROTHERS

"Raam! Check this out."

My open locker door bangs me square in the forehead as I turn to hear a loud, familiar voice roaring through the crowd, yelling my name through the hallway.

The sharp pain stings, and I feel I'm concussed—or, at least, my skull must be cracked open like an egg. A second later, the internal buzzing subsides, and Cake barrels through a group of students, pointing his cell phone at me.

"Watch," he says, pressing the phone into my face. He shouldn't have a phone in the open. We aren't allowed to use them at school outside of emergencies. Mine's in my bag.

Cake breathes heavily, and his eyes bulge. Sweat drips from his faux-hawk Sonic hairdo. Since kindergarten, he's been my best friend, and I've never seen him this worked up.

It's the last day of sixth grade, and I should be throwing away a year's worth of junk. All our lockers must be cleaned out before the end of the day. The inside of mine resembles one of those hoarder houses on reality TV. If Mom or Dad could see how messy it is, they'd ground me for life.

I get distracted by Reena Kapadia taking selfies with her best friends across the hall. I'll miss her sitting behind me in World Cultures, where she'd occasionally tap my shoulder to borrow a pencil. My fingers begin to tingle as I rub the back of my neck.

"Stop gawking," Cake says, folding his arms across his chest. "This is more important."

Reluctantly, I grab the phone from him.

"Watch the video," he demands. The dude is all business.

I hit the play button.

Though it's loud in the open-air hallway with everyone celebrating their freedom from school, I can hear dramatic background music playing through the phone speaker. The screen has tricked-out filters and graphics like I'm watching a summer blockbuster trailer. A ball bounces, and a plume of smoke fills the screen. The face of my favorite player, Aron

Hardaway, appears, and a message shows up like a *Star Wars* crawl.

BREAKING NEWS:

Aron Hardaway appearing at Hoop Con

The video swipes to Hardaway. He smiles as he talks to the camera.

"I'm excited to be a guest at Hoop Con this June. I'm looking forward to hanging out with all the kids and, most importantly, everyone having fun and shooting hoops. Sign up soon and get a chance to meet me."

And then, it cuts out with a link to the website.

I slowly turn to Cake, who waggles his eyebrows.

"Is this a joke?" I ask, stunned. "Wasn't he in Europe shooting a movie?"

"Nope," he confirms. "And I just got my passes to Hoop Con."

"No way," I say.

"One of my dad's patients hooked it up," he says proudly.

Of course, both of Cake's parents are doctors.

"You gotta get yours, man."

"Dude, I'm trying. The last time I checked, they were sold

out, and some of the ticket sites were selling them at five hundred dollars a pop."

"Talk to your parents again," Cake says. He puts his phone into his pocket.

"I have," I say, gritting my teeth.

Hoop Con is a five-day basketball extravaganza at the Orange County Convention Center in Orlando. It's the Comic-Con for ballers: the ultimate immersive, interactive experience with thirteen different basketball-related activities, including dunk contests, shooting competitions, live games, autograph and photograph sessions, exhibits, brand activations, and an e-sports lounge. They are hosting camps so kids have the opportunity to brush up on their skills. There was already a robust list of current and former players, and now that Aron will be there, I must figure out how I'd get to go.

Half the students at school wear #33 Hardaway Orlando Magic jerseys, including me. Let's be clear. There is no more prominent name in the game today. Aron Hardaway has been in the league for only two years, and he's won the dunk and three-point contest and made the All-Star Game each season. He can do it all. Shoot, defend, dish the rock, and hit the glass. He's also the size of Giannis with Kyrie's handles and Steph's range. I even have a Slam of Da Month poster of him in my locker next to the little silver Krishna statue Mom gave me for good luck.

He had the dopest sneaker line ever. Each release is a huge event. We signed up for his last pair, Sky Hardaway Slam High District 13s, but missed getting them. Aron has endorsement deals with everyone from auto insurance to crypto to sports drinks, where he showcases his trademark grin. He even has a martial arts video game where you battle all sorts of demons, goblins, and zombies for interdimensional domination.

I once saw Aron at a gas station when he peeled out in his souped-up Ferrari. It was the most incredible car I'd ever seen.

I grab a basketball from my locker. It needs air, but I spin it in my hands, imagining schooling everyone in my new Sky Hardaway kicks. When Reena passes by in her red dress and tells me to have a great vacation, I barely notice in time to wave.

Cake lunges over and grabs a nutrition bar I was about to throw away among old candy wrappers and scraps of homework.

"The date's expired," I warn him.

"Yeah, six months ago," he says as he rips the wrapper and takes a bite. "Still edible."

Before I can intervene, he eats the whole thing.

"Stale, yet chewy," he says, initially shaking his head before slowly nodding in acceptance. This guy will eat anything.

The bus ride home is festive, and it's the last day Cake and I will be stuck in the front seats. The seventh and eighth graders fill the middle and back, but the Moore brothers, Justin and Dustin, are no longer here to torment us. They got suspended for throwing eggs out the window at passing cars, not to mention how often they pegged us with rubber bands and erasers. Now, they're home on an early vacation. And I won't have to deal with them again until next year.

Everyone is exuberant; even our bus driver smiles, despite getting paper balls thrown at him—probably happy to be rid of us.

Cake and I live in this large neighborhood called Storybrook West, located a few miles down the road. It's got a golf course that's been closed for a year now. Dad says a developer is trying to build condos. He's still upset because he hasn't used his new clubs, which gather dust in our garage.

Nobody's home when I walk in. Mom is still at her new dance studio and Dad's at some new hotel property where he handles video marketing. As of late, they've both spent more time away from home.

When I get inside, I notice Mom has left a snack of puris and sugar cookies for me in the kitchen. The dishes pile up in the sink, and Mom's chai cup is half full. I grab a couple of puris and cookies and go into my room, passing by the framed and garlanded photo of Apple Dada, Mom's dad, my late grandfather, who died about a year ago.

If my locker was a mess, my room is worse. I have clothes and shoes everywhere. On my walls hang posters of Aron, Steph, Giannis, Luka, and Jordan, my laundry hoop basket, a court rug on the floor, and a basketball-shaped light on the ceiling. I also have my mini hoop attached to the door on which I practice my dunks. At four foot eight, I still can't touch the net on a regulation rim. I skimmed it with my finger last month. Close, but not yet. On this rim, however, I'm a dunking god.

I check my computer. My other set of grandparents, my dad's parents, are visiting India for the summer, and they emailed me photos from their vacation in Rajasthan. The funny thing is they live ten minutes away from us, but they spend half the year hanging in the motherland. My dad said my grandparents came to America when they were still teens, so they are making up for years of being homesick. Usually, I'd hang out at their house after school.

Dad grew up in Orlando, and the proximity to family is one of the reasons my parents moved from California when I was two. I was born in Los Angeles, though I don't remember it.

My cousin Trina still lives there. She's the closest thing to a sister that I have. And she's asked me to visit a few times. For some reason, Mom and Dad haven't been back. Not sure why. Trina keeps telling me about these incredible food spots, the basketball, and the weather. LA seems awesome.

I skip the attached photo album and check the Hoop Con website to see if the Aron announcement is authentic. Indeed, his headshot and the news appear on the home page. I quickly go to Ticket Hub to see if any Hoop Con tickets are available. Since Aron's confirmation, they've doubled in price. I must convince my parents I need to go no matter the cost. Even individual day passes are sold out.

I pull my phone out of my bag. Unlike Cake's latest smartphone, mine is three years old, a hand-me-down from my parents. It's cracked, chipping, and flips. I need to get some advice. I hit up Trina. She's a heck of a baller.

ME: **School is ova! You hear Aron's gonna be at Hoop Con?**

TRINA: **DUUUUDE, I still have a week. NO WAY. That's awesome. You going?**

ME: **Passes are like $500. I asked Mom and Dad about it. They were hesitant. And that's when prices were half that.**

TRINA: **Keep talking to them. Something will work out. How's your game?**

ME: **Good. Mastering that dribble.**

TRINA: **Sweet. I'm still at school :(Message me later.**

ME: **Cool.**

Let me clarify: Trina's not technically my cousin. She's my aunt. Her dad, Mahendra Uncle, and my grandfather, Apple Dada, were brothers. Yeah, it's a little confusing. She and my mom are first cousins. But Trina and I are only two years apart, probably because her dad and my grandfather are twenty years apart. Trina always likes to pull seniority over me and make me address her as Trina Masi when we are around others.

My parents are lukewarm about my basketball obsession. I get solid grades, yet they want me to concentrate on other academic pursuits like Gujarati classes, coding, and the spelling bee. Dad's not going to be thrilled I got a B plus in Reading.

Cake texts me.

CAKE: **Highlight time?**

ME: **Heck, yeah.**

I pump air into my basketball. The ball loses its bounce after so many mornings and afternoon games at school. The grip has worn down to a nub.

I change into shorts and a T-shirt and my Hardaways. I have a couple of pairs, just not the costly ones.

I hear a ball's *ka-thump* on the backyard sidewalk a few minutes later. Cake lives directly across from me on the eighth hole, which now looks like a jungle of overgrown foliage. His house is three stories, and he's got a sweet game room and a pool. It's twice the size of mine.

Cake's real name is Chirag, but since his sixth birthday, when he ate every variety of cheesecake from Cheesecake Factory like it was a hot-dog eating competition, I've called him Cake. Only his mom calls him Chirag.

When I get to the porch, Cake flees from a large bird that looks like a dinosaur. His hands flap around in panic.

Since the golf course shut down a year ago, our backyard has become a zoo. We've had various guests come and visit, ranging from rabbits, coyotes, snakes, and bobcats to the occasional alligator looking for a place under the sun. We also had a black bear who would rummage through trash cans and break into a few houses. He's reclusive, and we never found him, even though residents would post home surveillance videos of him on the neighborhood Facebook page.

There's one specific group of birds known as sandhill cranes specializing in harassing Cake every time he comes over.

He manages to slip through the screen door before the bird pecks parts of his flesh.

"Man, this place is Jurassic Park," he says, hands on his hips and catching his breath.

We wait a few minutes until the bird flies away and then we exit. The aluminum screen door slams shut behind us.

The basketball court is a block away near the clubhouse and pool area. We also have ponds and a lake nearby where you can fish. The weather is late May—hot and muggy and typical

Florida. Cake's already drenched in perspiration, and I wipe my forehead. But we're free—three months of fun, sun, and balling all day ahead of us.

"Did you get passes?" Cake asks as he searches around for the bird.

"Not yet," I say. "Parents aren't home yet."

"Dude, you have to go. I hear Aron's doing a sneaker drop."

"No way," I say.

"Yeah, his last pairs sold for one thousand dollars."

"I want to rock them on my own feet," I say.

As we walk, I practice the reverse cross-step drill I saw in Aron's Master School video series. I'm not sure how he does it. I'm improving my version of it. Cake serves as my victim.

"You know Aron is also doing a clinic during one of the camp sessions."

"Tickets are like five hundred dollars now since he announced this afternoon. And that's only for a day pass."

"Worth every penny."

For Cake, probably. His dad drives a brand-new Tesla.

Of us two, I'm the playmaker and scorer, and he's the forward and enforcer. Crazy, we used to be the same height, but he

12

went through a vertical and horizontal growth spurt this year, and I'm still waiting for mine. One of our teachers laughed at us once and called us Laurel and Hardy. I had to look that one up. Whatever. I know I'm short and wiry, but I know my skills, man. And Cake might joke when he calls himself the round mound of rebound, but he's sneaky agile and will make you look stupid if you underestimate him.

"That's a fresh move," Cake says, taking out his phone. "I have to get that on my channel."

Earlier this year, Cake started his hoop handle on Instagram called Slice of Cake. He posts highlights, mash-ups, and as of late, trick shots.

He's obsessed with growing his audience. He does all his editing on his phone using all sorts of apps. I have no idea how. We team up together for ideas. He got a new gimbal that allows him to shoot cool angles of our plays.

"Did you see the latest?" Cake asks. "I'm up to four hundred followers."

"That's great," I say.

"It's improving," he says, disappointed. "The kid from Court Kings hit seventy thousand yesterday."

"You'll get there," I reassure him.

While he's worried about followers, I'm obsessed with who's the best in our class. I know all the top players from fifth through twelfth grade.

"You see, Payton Newman is the number-one sixth grader in Florida now?" I tell him. "He scored forty points in his last AAU game."

I saw Payton play a few months ago at a prep tournament downtown. He had some moves, but I think he's overhyped. Could I take him? You bet I can.

"We got this summer to improve our skills," Cake says. "And make the team next year."

The sun finally dips behind a cluster of clouds, giving us much-needed shade.

Cake and I tried out for the middle school team last year. We made it to the last cut but didn't make the final roster. Sure, we were sixth graders, but it stung because I knew we were good enough. I don't think Coach Demer, the head coach, likes me much. He kept saying I should pass more, even though I know I'm one of the best shooters in the school. Why would I not use my best skill? I don't think I ever got over that burn of getting cut.

"At least we got Y-ball starting in July," I say.

Cake and I are playing in the YMCA league. We signed up as teammates. We've played on the same team since we were seven.

"Spice Brothers back together," we both say, laughing.

I'm Spice Curry, and Cake dubs himself Clay Oven. We garam like dat!

We pass a flagpole surrounded by flowers. The American flag flaps back and forth. I hear splashing and screaming from people swimming and diving at the community pool. I used to love going to the splash pad as a kid until the whole area was shut down for a week because someone had peed in it.

We approach the court. It's empty.

Usually, we stretch, warm up, and run drills. Today it's way too hot. My shirt is already soaked like a sponge. We get right to business.

We've seen all the trick-shot videos online, and most use visual effects. Cake and I are purists.

For the next hour, we will try everything. Bounce shots, behind the goal, long hook, through the legs, half-court, sitting down, backward. You name it, and we'll attempt it.

Cake will record, slice, and dice it together with a dope beat and unleash it on the internet.

I take a few jumpers and then try a backward granny shot that ricochets badly off the backboard and onto the grass near the parking lot. I run up to retrieve it when a souped-up golf cart that looks like a monster truck pulls up. The Moore brothers, Justin and Dustin, hop off. Instead of tossing the ball back like a decent human being, Justin kicks it farther. Jerk.

I can't stand them. Justin would trip me at school, bump me from behind at lunch, spill my food tray, and even stuff me in a locker.

When I finally return with the ball, they have already taken over the court. They grab Cake's gimbal and phone and make him chase them around the court to retrieve them.

I might be shorter and skinnier than the Moore twins, but I still won't take their crap.

"Give him back his phone," I say. "We were here first."

"You scrubs need to go," Justin says, laughing. They grow weird facial hair that looks like a lab experiment gone wrong.

"Time for the elders to play," Dustin says.

"We aren't leaving."

The Moores wander over to try to intimidate us. Yes, they are bigger than us by a foot and have mustaches, but they have a combined IQ equal to half a rock.

"Want to make a bet you will?" Dustin says.

"Why don't you play us?" I ask. I narrow my eyes.

Cake clutches his jersey and yanks at it.

"Haha, yeah, right." Justin grunts out loud. "You need to hit a certain size to play us."

He holds his hand low to the ground like he's measuring me for an amusement park ride height requirement.

"Afraid we can beat you?" I sneer.

"Want me to stuff you into a locker again in front of your girlfriend?" Justin says.

Cold-blooded. I couldn't look Reena in the eyes for a month. I was so embarrassed.

"Losers leave for the rest of the summer," I say, cracking my knuckles.

"Fine," Dustin says. "This should be easy."

Justin and Dustin play for the school team. They beat us badly before. This time we're better, quicker, and more motivated.

We agree on the rules.

Standard: Play to 11. Win by 2. Make it, take it.

We shoot for the ball.

I take the shot, and it rims out.

Justin chucks it and somehow banks it in. He sticks his hand in my face.

"Kiss my glass."

I ignore him and set up on defense.

"Check the ball," he says.

I shove it at him, biting the inside of my cheek.

Cake guards Dustin. He looks like he's sagging. I offer him a reassuring nod.

You can't tell the Moores apart, except Dustin has brown hair and Justin has ice-blond like a Malfoy.

Justin dribbles, and I play ironclad defense. I know how to get in front of him. He elbows me in the chest. The blow takes the wind out of me, and he scores on a layup.

Dustin misses a jumper on the next possession, and Cake grabs the rebound. He hits me with a bounce pass and sets a pick and roll. I dish it back to him for what should be an easy layup until Justin karate chops him across the arms.

"Foul," Cake says, holding his wrist. "You almost hacked my hand off."

"No broke, no croak," Justin says.

I can see the red imprint of a palm on Cake's wrist.

On the next possession, I make a clean strip. And they call a foul.

"Seriously, all ball," I groan.

Justin jumps up and down like he's been scarred for life.

Give these guys an Oscar. They need applause for this acting performance.

They score quickly on the next few possessions using the strange bond twins seemingly share. They communicate tele-pathically on plays and confuse Cake and me on defense. We find ourselves down 8–1 and huffing and puffing in the scorch-ing sun.

Cake and I get a break when the ball gets tipped out of bounds. It's time for us to regroup. We have been down this scenario previously and know how to make tweaks.

"It's time to rain," I say, tossing my hands up and down.

That's our bat signal. He nods his head. We know what to do. We lack a size advantage. Our strength lies on the outside, especially for me. I got more range than a Rover when it comes to the perimeter.

Cake and I use the pick and pop. Cake drills two jumpers, and we gain steam.

When the Moores adjust to our tactic, we take them out of the paint. I channel my inner Steph and drain a long three. Tie game.

Of course, I rub it in their faces with a "we are cooking" gesture.

Cake scores on the next play with a nifty finger roll off the glass. We're up one.

"Icing on the cake," he boasts, pumping his fist.

I wish he got that on video.

All we need now is another basket. The Moores play us tight, their mouths twist. I end up with an opening. I execute Hardaway's double-cross maneuver, which surprises even me. Cross. Jab. And then a lane opens up, and I drive in for an easy layup.

Cake daps me up in celebration before driving another basket home. Another one bites the dust.

"Doesn't count," Justin says. "I already called time-out."

He rubs his eye.

"My contact was stuck."

"No way, we win," I yell. "You don't even wear contacts."

"It's a do-over," Dustin demands.

"We won fair and square," Cake says.

Both the twins approach us like they want to fight. They pound their fists.

"You want to try that again, punks?" Justin blusters, nostrils flaring.

Beating them in basketball is something I know we can do. Fighting them, not so much. Not that I didn't want a shot.

Cake is bigger than me, but these guys are enormous.

"Fine, we'll do it again," Cake says.

I side-eye Cake, but that's fine. We did it once. We can do it again.

I recheck the ball to Justin. I pass to Cake. He dishes it back to me. I pivot and start my dribble. Justin flanks me on my left side. No prob. This is my moment to shine. I'm going to light him up. I put the ball through my legs and back out from the three-point line. Justin creeps up. I once saw Aron do this open crossover where he pretended to go in one direction and let the ball float in the air while accelerating the other way. It wasn't your typical crossover. There was this magic moment, and he savaged his defender with a dunk. I will do the same thing to Justin but nail a three.

So I pretend to point my chest in Cake's direction, but then I cross over low and explode. Except Justin doesn't fall for it. I end up getting trapped in the baseline corner. Dustin comes over to double-team and trap me. Cake waves frantically for me to pass it to him. But nothing against him, I'm going to hit this shot. I end up idiotically picking up my dribble. I rise and try to pump-fake those guys. I chuck the ball up and watch a high arc that hits the front of the rim and somehow bounces right into Cake's hands. Except he dribbles the ball right off his knee out of bounds. I throw up my hands in frustration.

"Dude, how did you not catch that?!" I yell at Cake.

He looks at me frustrated, his hands raised.

"I was wide open," he says.

"Yeah, you should have caught that."

"I'm talking about the shot you took. I kept signaling at you."

"I must have missed it."

"You did. You shouldn't have picked up your dribble."

I'm getting frustrated by Cake's lecture.

"Bro, learn how to grab a rebound."

We both go silent and glare at each other. I don't like to lose.

The Moores tell us to hurry up. They are both laughing.

Cake and I are both livid. This game should be over by now.

On the following play, I check the ball back to Justin. He takes two steps forward and picks up his dribble. I try to strip it. He somehow gets the ball to his brother, who fires a rainbow three over Cake. The ball hits the backboard and goes in.

The Moores raise their hands. I shake my head in disbelief. I grimace at Cake. He should have caught that rebound. It was right there, and now we lost.

Justin gets in my face trying to intimidate me.

"See ya, chumps," he says, waving us away.

"You know we won," I say.

"Na, na, na, hey, hey. Go whine to your mom," Dustin says. "This is our court."

"Give me my ball back," I say.

Justin realizes he holds my basketball in his hands. He smirks. Then he takes the ball and kicks it high and far. The ball bounces near the pond's shore and into the water with a splash.

My head pounds in anger, and I'm about to deck Justin.

I lunge at him. Cake grabs me from behind.

"Yo, we'll get it back," he says.

I'm fuming.

"Oops." Justin yawns. "Did I do that?"

He laughs hysterically and walks away.

"No point arguing with them," Cake says as we walk back home. "They lack intelligence, and we lack muscle mass. Plus, you have to sign up for Hoop Con."

I'm shadowboxing. He's right. However, one day I'm going to teach Justin a lesson.

Before I go back inside, Cake taps me on the shoulder.

"Raam, you got to trust others to play as well," he says. "Trust your teammates. I was open. You should have passed me the ball."

I don't say anything back. I'm still upset and now annoyed. I rub my brow. I'm getting a headache. No one takes the last shot but me. Not even Cake. I'm the only person I can trust at that moment.

BALLE, BALLE

Mom's home when I get back.

"Alexa," she says from the kitchen. "Play 'Chunari, Chunari.'"

She's wearing workout pants and a top and loading the dishwasher. Her large green eyes follow me like one of those Egyptian hieroglyph paintings of Cleopatra you find inside pyramids. Her hair is tied in Princess Leia buns. I can see a sprout of silver among her thick black hair.

A harmonium, a drum bass, followed by a Bollywood beat, pumps through the speakers. Mom makes strange facial movements like a bobblehead and then starts to dance and lip-synch the song's lyrics. She twirls and throws her hands up. She smiles at me, grabs a dish towel, puts it around my neck, and tries to get me to dance with her. I escape as quickly as I can.

"You don't like the new steps?" she asks.

"No, it's creepy," I remark.

"You used to love dancing with me when you were young. Remember this song?"

"No," I say.

I'm lying. I know the song and the movie. It's ingrained in my psyche. I also know if I said yes, Mom would go into our Bollywood backstory. She was an actress in India. The Jen A of Bombay, she likes to say. Whatever that means.

She finishes dancing. She teaches a Bollywood dance class and choreography lessons for Indian parents who aspire for their kids to be the next Priyanka.

"So, how was the last day of sixth grade?" she asks.

"It was fine," I say, scratching my throat.

"My sweet boy is growing up."

She tries to hug me. I'm sweating. She quickly lets go, wrinkling her nose.

"And he needs to shower."

The sharp pain of losing to the Moores fills my head with rage. Hoop Con will have several clinics and practice sessions and a skills academy. I need to be there if I want to beat the

Moores and make the team. And now Aron's going. I have to go. It's imperative. All this rushes back as I see Mom.

"Did you know Aron Hardaway is going to be at Hoop Con?" I beg her. "Can I please go?"

Mom stares at me. Her eyes swirl with the colors of the ocean, but around them, I notice dark circles like a shore. It's like she's in a trance.

"That's exciting," she says distractedly. "We'll discuss it with your dad."

"You guys have been saying that for weeks," I say. "Where is he now?"

"At the new hotel," Mom says, staring outside. "They are breaking ground today. Vipul Uncle wanted to make a big show of it."

Dad works in a hospitality and travel company owned by Vipul Desai. Vipul Uncle owns a chain of motels and hotels on International Drive and South Florida. Dad likes to joke that he's a member of the Patel Motel Cartel. Dad helps run the content and video department. Working for Vipul Uncle isn't fun. Dad constantly complains that he has other dreams.

My parents are both of Indian origin, but Dad was born in

27

New Jersey and raised in Orlando. Mom was born and bred in Mumbai. They started talking online before they even met. They're not only geographically different but also in their personalities too.

I notice the puffy, pale indentation on Mom's ring finger. No band.

"He says he'll be back today," Mom says. "I brought your favorite butter chicken from Amrit's Palace to celebrate your last day."

I notice the brown bag and the incredible aroma wafting through the kitchen.

Dad's been sleeping in the guest room for the last few months. As of late, he's been away at work more than he's been home.

As another filmi song plays, I hear the garage door open. A second later, Dad walks through the door.

He hasn't shaved. Gray stubble covers his face. He's sifting through mail on the counter. I notice he wears his ring.

He looks surprised to see both of us.

"Hey, Dad," I say. "Guess what?"

"Hey, Raam." He sighs.

He stares at Mom and takes another breath.

"Hi, Tanuja," he says.

"Hi, Naresh," she says. "I got butter chicken from Amrit's Palace."

They are both quiet. I need to bring up Hoop Con now. I can't wait any longer.

"Dad," I say. "Aron Hardaway is coming to Hoop Con. Can I go? You said you'd think about it."

My dad regards me like I'm some strange alien. His mind is elsewhere. It's like he got frozen on a bad Zoom connection.

"What is the cost?" he finally asks.

It's always the cost.

"Five hundred dollars."

"How much?!"

Now, I have his attention—even Mom tugs at her earring.

"Five hundred dollars. Prices are going up since Aron announced he's going—"

"To play basketball?" he asks. He rolls his eyes.

"Well, that and more," I say. "They're doing shooting drills, tournaments, and exhibits. A bunch of players will be there, and all my friends are going."

"What about coding classes or spelling bee camp?" Dad asks.

He grabs an envelope and tears it open with his teeth.

"Yes, Raam," Mom says. "At the mandir, they are doing a camp for all the kids. Imagine you could be competing in the competition on TV next year?"

I look at her, incredulous.

"Everyone is going to be at Hoop Con."

Dad glances at the contents of the letter and stares up at me, waving it in my face.

"See, this is a four-hundred-dollar electric bill. I'm not paying five hundred dollars for you to play a silly sport and get some autographs. I don't care if Michael Jordan or LeBron James will be there and they give you bars of gold. You need to concentrate on your academics and future. Not some silly dream of playing in the NBA."

"Aron is better than both," I say.

My dad laughs as he rips up the letter and tosses it into the trash can.

"You never saw either play in their prime," he says dismissively. "Also, aren't you playing YMCA basketball next month? I think that's enough basketball for one summer."

"Can't I just go for a few days?" I ask.

Mom brushes her hair back and looks at me, tilting her head.

Dad's phone buzzes. Mom looks at us with a tight-lipped smile.

"Okay," he says into the phone, crossing his arms. "Okay. Fine. I'll be there soon. Yes, I'm leaving now."

Mom's face drops. Dad's face flushes red. He grabs the pile of mail and slaps it on the counter with exasperation. His face tightens. He's gone from tired to frustrated, his usual pendulum of emotions.

"We can discuss this later," he sternly tells us. "There's a new performance by stilt walkers in the lobby that must be captured. It's always a matter of life or death for Vipul."

He leaves, slamming the door to the garage. Mom stares blankly at it for a few seconds, then back to me. I gnaw at the inside of my mouth.

"Let me see if I can work something out," she says, bobbing her head.

I ignore her. She could have spoken up before.

"Sure, Mom, whatever," I say.

"Are you going to eat?" Mom asks as I walk to my room, leaving her alone. "I don't want this food to go cold."

I don't answer. The garlic and lemon smell of the

chicken is tempting, but I lost my appetite a while ago.

I plop onto my bed and text Trina again.

ME: **parents still stalling. They want me to go to spelling bee camp. Not sure what to do.**

TRINA: **bummer. don't depend on anyone. Take initiative if u really want to go.**

ME: **I got it.**

TRINA: **u do.**

ME: **yeah.**

If my parents don't want to pay for it, I will.

I don't have a job or a stock portfolio, and the piggy bank I do have only has enough cash to pay for a large Domino's pizza.

So now I have to raise at least five hundred bucks. I have only one choice. I look under my bed and pull a shoebox out. Inside there's a thick plastic slab with a card. My Panini Prizm Patch Aron Hardaway rookie refractor. It's a one of twenty-five and has a piece of his uniform. It's my prize possession. It's also the most valuable thing I own. The result of five years of birthday, Diwali, and Christmas money saved. It's the rainy day fund.

I get online and check eBay. Mom went through a phase where she imported Indian handbags, purses, and clutches and sold them on Etsy and eBay. She had me list them. We sold a few but, after a month, abandoned the scheme. I still had her account information. I promise I didn't use it for anything nefarious.

The comps tell me the card is selling for around five hundred dollars. I reluctantly list it as a buy-now option. I can't wait for an auction.

If I can sell the card, I can afford my pass to Hoop Con. Each day the price seems to get more expensive for passes. I do what I need to do.

TWO WEEKS LATER

Hoop Con starts tomorrow. My card still hasn't sold.

Dad made me enroll in this spelling bee camp after discovering my subpar reading grade. Mom insists she has something brewing. I doubt it. The fact is the price for the event skyrocketed on all the ticket websites for day and week passes.

I'm sitting in one of the Hindu temple classrooms with other kids doing spelling bee drills. I don't know how many multisyllable words, alternate pronunciations, and languages of origin I can take. I hear the Sanskrit mantras being sung over the speakers in the main hall. Murtis and paintings of the Hindu gods like Ganesh, Krishna, and Shiva decorate the walls. They would be an excellent 3-on-3 team.

At least when we'd come to the temple during religious events, Cake and I could sneak out and take shots on the hoop in the back. Now, it's gone.

I'm bored. And it's only been the first day. Our teacher, Nupur Auntie, keeps reminding us that spelling is F-U-N! She might say that, but she runs that camp like a drill instructor. She's sent four kids to the National Spelling Bee in DC, and her course is like one of those top college football schools that cranks out first-round picks every year.

In the first practice bee, I misspelled *ubiquitous*. I was the first person eliminated. The girl next to me got it right. Ask her to spell *Giannis Antetokounmpo*. I bet you she couldn't do it. I could.

Thankfully, the first day is over. Mom picks me up. She smiles at me when I buckle up in the front seat and winks.

"Guess who's going to Hoop Con tomorrow?" Mom asks.

I stare back at her, wide-eyed.

"No freaking way," I say.

She tosses me a new basketball.

"Yeah, way," she says, smiling. "And it's the weeklong pass."

"How?" I ask. "The prices are astronomical."

"Oh, your mom has her ways," she teases, patting my hand.

I stare at the ball like a sacred object representing all my hopes and dreams.

I give her a hug, which surprises her and me.

"Thanks, Mom!" I say.

I'm almost in tears from the surprise. I haven't gotten a gift like this since my ninth birthday when I got my first pair of Sky Hardaways.

I let Mom go.

"Seriously, how did you pull this off?" I ask, genuinely curious.

"I'm a Bombay girl," she says, eyes twinkling. "I know how to wheel and deal. It also doesn't hurt that Kalpana Auntie's son-in-law works for the Magic and needs someone to give his daughter Arangetram lessons."

She starts the car.

"What are you going to do about the spelling bee camp? You already paid for it."

"That five hundred dollars you made on eBay can cover it."

"Wait, what?" I ask, flummoxed. "It sold?"

"What did you sell?"

"The Aron card."

"You loved that card . . ."

Well, Mom knows. I should have known better. At least, someone bought it. The bad news is the buyer probably made way more. It's bittersweet.

"The good news is I made some money and can pay you back," I say.

Mom puts her hand on mine.

"That's sweet. But I'm only kidding. Classes at the mandir are free. We can figure out another way you can use that money, Mr. Millionaire."

She laughs and peels out of the parking lot, tires screeching. The ball pops out of my hand, and I grip the door handle.

"Sorry. Sometimes I still think I'm driving in India."

"Did you tell Dad?" I ask, curious to see whether he approved.

She looks in the rearview, adjusting her sunglasses.

"Didn't get a chance. He went to Miami for a few days to check out the new hotel Vipul Uncle was building."

"Got it."

I didn't want to ask as long as I got one parent to agree. And the less Dad knows, the better.

I regain my equilibrium as we merge onto the highway. I grab the ball and turn it around in my hand, feeling the fresh new leather smoothness. My destiny is about to change. I can't wait to tell Cake. Mom cranks more Bollywood music. I'm ready to balle, balle.

I text Cake and Trina as soon as I get home.

ME: **Bruh, guess who's coming to Hoop Con!?!!?**

CAKE: **Wutttttt? How?**

ME: **Momma dukes hooked it up**

TRINA: **Suhweeet**

I put my phone down and start watching Aron's highlights. I've studied every aspect of his game, from his crossover to jab step jelly and techniques and how he shoots using the back of the net. I try some of his moves out on the hoop on my door. I drill my fadeaway jumper. Smooth like dat. Tomorrow I'll be doing it for real.

HOOP CON

I've been staring at the upside-down house for five straight minutes. It's the WonderWorks building, an interactive amusement park we went to for an elementary school field trip that featured such bizarre science experiments as the Earthquake Café, Hurricane Shack, and the Bed of Nails. We're half a mile away from the convention center. I'm in Mom's minivan, and we've lurched down International Drive, the famous tourist street full of hotels, time-shares, chain restaurants, mini-golf courses, and water parks, for what feels like an hour.

I tap the ball with my fingers and spin it in my hand. I made sure we left early enough. But it's 8:25, and the event starts in five minutes. Waiting feels like standing in line at Space

Mountain. Mom cranes her neck out the window, and I do the same, to see rows of cars turning into the convention center parking garage.

"I don't see any accidents," Mom observes. "There are some news vans. Maybe the president is here?"

"Mom, the president isn't as popular as Aron," I joke. "He didn't average a triple-double and win MVP in his second year."

She laughs and snorts. I haven't seen her do that in a while.

The car still doesn't move. I notice other kids leaving their vehicles and walking toward the convention center entrance, dribbling balls and clutching book bags.

The convention center is a giant complex composed of two buildings connected by a sky bridge. They have all sorts of events there. Dad took me there when I was in fourth grade to check out a car show where I got to sit in a Lamborghini, and Mom once took me to an Indian wedding expo. No, she wasn't trying to plan my wedding. She was looking for clients.

A giant sign on the marquee outside the building promotes Hoop Con. They even have an action photo of Aron.

My head rushes with paranoia. I'm going to be late. I unstrap my belt. And grab my ball.

"Mom, I gotta go," I say, opening the door.

Her jaw drops, and her hand suddenly grabs me like I'm about to jump out of a plane without a parachute.

"What are you doing?" she asks, flabbergasted. "We're still driving. This is a busy intersection."

I point to the other kids.

"Line's not moving. I'm going to be late."

We're trapped. Mom looks around and relents.

"Okay," she says. "Be careful."

Mom leans over and kisses me on the cheek. I rub the lipstick off as quickly as I can.

"Have fun," she says as I open the door and leap out. Mom rolls down the window.

"Kick butt today!" she shouts. I wave back.

I bounce the ball on the sidewalk and run toward the Grand Concourse entrance. My stomach is churning, and my head feels light—the clock's ticking. There are media crews, equipment vans, and police everywhere navigating traffic.

There's a massive neon HOOP CON sign glowing in front of the doorway. I enter through the automatic doors and ascend a long escalator to the second floor. In front of me are crowds of fans and other kids. All of them are decked out in basketball gear. There must be thousands of people. Most of them, though, wear Aron jerseys.

A swarm of media and crowds of fans surround the place. When I finally get off the escalator, another long line awaits me at the entrance, where we have to register and pick up our badges. The whole place has a funky tropical look with seashell sculptures and fake palm trees.

Maybe I'm at a carnival. There's a tailgate atmosphere, like when Dad used to take me to Florida Gator football games in Gainesville. We would barbecue with his old roommates and play cornhole while they would talk about what five-star cornerback they recruited and how much they hated Georgia. Mom enjoyed it, and I loved eating hot dogs and wearing my Tim Tebow jersey.

When I make my way to the registration, I join a line stretching out the door. Inside the convention center, loud bass music throbs from speakers.

There are people of every shape and size, some dribbling, others with headphones and backpacks, and even others doing live broadcasts for different countries. I see one dude with

Aron's number and face shaved into his scalp. He couldn't be older than ten. One girl even brought her dog, which wears a customized Hardaway jersey around its body.

They all look like they are going to one of those comic cosplay conventions where everyone dresses up as their favorite superhero. For all of us, that figure would be Aron Hardaway. We are hoop nerds trying to squeeze through the double doors for a once-in-a-lifetime chance.

Camera crews record everything. Some look like news media outlets. Others look like they are part of the Hoop Con crew because they all sport the same polos.

I search the crowd, trying to find Cake. About twenty feet away, the Moore twins harass another kid by playing keep-away with his ball. A bolt of anger runs through me. Yet, now is not the time to worry about them.

I spot others from my school like Patrick Fiesta, who we call Beast. He's the quiet kid in class, but on the court, he goes into full beast mode. I also see Eddie Turner, who we call ET because all he does is talk about alien encounters.

Hesh and Anup are also here. Both of these guys are cousins who are also our crosstown Indian rivals. Hesh is tolerable, unlike Anup. We call Anup "One-Up" because he has to one-up you on everything, no matter how trivial: Sneakers, cars, houses, music. Anup is about being better than you. These two also happen to be cousins with Reena, putting me in an awkward situation that Cake loves to exploit.

Finally, Cake appears. He's hobnobbing with some random campers I don't know. His Sonic faux-hawk has now transformed into a buzz cut with faded lines. Cake is like the mayor, constantly chattering and networking. He has a media business to run. I bounce my ball off his back to get his attention. He turns around, looking annoyed.

"Dude, not cool," Cake says, rubbing his back as if I maimed him.

He dons the special Alt-City Aron jersey they only gave during games. His parents have season tickets.

"I heard from this kid," he says, pointing, "who heard from his mom's boyfriend that Aron is debuting his new dunk. Also, I met the guy who manages all of Aron's social media. I told him about my handle."

"No way," I say, scanning the onslaught of endless faces.

The line starts to pick up. Security checks us through a

metal detector. All of them are the size of NFL linebackers. They bust an old man who tries to sneak in. The guard grabs him by the shirt and tosses him out. These guys aren't joking around.

A group of college-age kids in Hoop Con polos are running check-in when I get to the kiosk.

They sit with laptops and clipboards and scramble in and out around the floor, yelling into walkie-talkies and headsets. The *oontz oontz* from the speakers reverberates loudly.

A girl with pigtails signals me to come forward. Cake heads to another registering area.

"No, we are out of the book bags," she says as I approach.

"Huh?"

"QR code?" she asks.

I show her my sign-in code on my phone. She scans it.

I survey the area. There is advertising, sponsor banners, and signs from clothing brands to NFTs everywhere I look.

She reaches to another table and hands me a drawstring tote with a Hoop Con logo.

"Here's your swag bag."

"Thanks," I say. "Do you know when Aron will be here?"

"As soon as possible," she says politely. "He's finishing shooting a commercial. Don't worry. He won't miss today for anything."

"Okay," I respond.

That's her default answer since every other participant is probably wondering the same.

"Have a great time, and don't forget to check out the shop for all your Hoop Con gear."

She's onto the next kid.

I grab my bag.

Cake strolls toward me, his hand already plucking out the gear like a rabbit from a hat.

"Bro, look at these threads," he says, holding up the Hoop Con jersey that's this trippy tie-dye blue color. "Fully reversible. Sick!"

There's a water bottle, socks, wristbands, basketball cards, applesauce, and a T-shirt. Cake pulls out a pair of kicks. They are brand-new limited-edition Aron Jet hightops with a Fruity Pebbles color scheme. They are the freshest sneakers I've ever seen. Cake smiles like he won the lottery.

"Did you win a contest or something?" I ask.

My ribs tighten as I take a deep breath.

"Nah, dude," Cake says nonchalantly. "I upgraded my experience when I signed up. You didn't see the options?"

Mom signed me up for the basic package. I pull out a T-shirt and a nutrition bar. The T-shirt could fit Shaq.

Cake opens up his new embroidered backpack. He pulls out a hoodie, socks, and more.

"I also got a personalized photo shoot," he says.

Great. He got all that, and I got a T-shirt that wouldn't even fit Aron.

An uncanny feeling overcomes me. I force a fake smile. I want to crawl into a shell.

I throw my bar back into my bag.

"If you aren't going to eat that, can I have it?" he asks.

"Really?"

I'm flabbergasted.

"What? I'm hungry."

There's a commotion at the door. We see Payton Newman coming through with his surfer haircut, wearing sunglasses and long shorts that dangle to his ankles. A camera crew is right behind him. Cake opens his bag and pulls out his camera and monopod.

"I have to capture this," he says, sprinting toward the crowd.

Payton Newman is a prodigy, and he's just three months older than I am. I am not exaggerating, although I think he's overrated. He scored 91 points in a game and has over a million followers on YouTube. He's been featured in Bleacher Report and on *SportsCenter* and been on *The Tonight Show*, where he dribbled three balls at a time and showed off his behind-the-back crossover and jab steps. Rumor has it he does one hundred free throws, two hundred floaters, and two hundred jump shots daily.

He has played varsity basketball since fifth grade. His dad is also there. He coaches Payton too. Payton goes to Lake Highland, a smaller school in downtown Orlando. He announced he had already gotten college offers from Duke and Michigan. I have my doubts.

His dad makes LaVar Ball seem sane. They have their own reality show too. It feels like we know all his family. His sister has a game too. Payton has handles, though. Cake and I have studied his game and once saw a quarter where he scored 20 points and made these tall tree kids look slow and old. He's wearing his trademark fluorescent socks. His dad lingers back on his phone. Trina isn't a fan. She thinks he's all show and his dad uses him for publicity.

A bunch of kids run up to him. Cake's a big fan of his but I have my reservations—a camera guy brushes by me. Before Cake gets to Payton, he slips by through the door into the labyrinth of the convention center, his crew following him.

Cake and I grab our bags and head inside. A real DJ spins tracks on a turntable.

When Cake and I enter, we pass through a locker room–like tunnel that's made to resemble a pro game. The lights dim, and the crowd noise increases. An announcer says our names.

"Introducing the point guard from the Orlando Magic, Raam Patel!"

Cake and I look at each other. We spin around and take everything in.

"They must have an AI chip on this badge," I say. "This is awesome."

After we get through, we enter another area resembling a real-life court with a large jumbotron hanging over us and music and signage.

I check the schedule on the app.

"They have five days of activities. Let's see what we want to do," I say, overwhelmed.

We see different basketball-related areas. Most of the clinics and shooting drills start after lunch. For the time being, we check out everything else.

This is supposed to be an event that celebrates the game's art, fashion, and technology.

We see a Hall of Fame exhibit with player jerseys, sneakers, and historical artifacts. An artist spray-painted a huge mural. There are tables made out of the hardwood floors of past championships being put up for auction. We take selfies at the photo booths set up to look like you're posing with the commissioner at the draft or winning the championship trophy. They even have Aron's #33 game-worn home jersey when he scored 71 points.

Combine-drill areas are set up where we check out our wingspans and verticals. We even shoot jumpers and practice slamming the ball at different heights.

At seven feet, I'm Vince Carter. At eight feet, I can lay up and touch the net. We even hit up an arcade area where we play the latest version of *B-Ball 3000*, where we try out a VR headset.

We pass the pop-up shop, which sells T-shirts, key chains, and all sorts of merch. All of it is way too expensive.

And there it is, glimmering like a treasure. The limited-edition kicks. A bunch of campers surround it, phones in hand, snapping photos.

"Yo, this is IG gold," Cake says as he approaches the sneaker exhibit. Aron's shoes are displayed like a museum gallery, all under glass. These are beyond one of a kind. They are pieces of art. One of his sneakers sold for a million dollars last year at an auction. Cake gets close to the glass to get a better look. A security officer taps him to lean back.

"Got it," he says, backing up and taking his shot.

"Everyone, please report to the West Concourse in five minutes for basketball clinic drills," someone announces over the loudspeakers.

Camp's about to start. Cake and I grin.

Showtime!

We start our trek to the other end of the convention center, cutting through a large trade show with booths and vendors selling cards and autograph memorabilia. Part of me wants to stop by to check the goods, but we're about to ball.

The West Concourse is a giant exhibition space converted to fit ten full-size basketball courts. It's like they crammed ten gyms into one massive ballroom. I already see droves of kids shooting baskets; the symphony of dozens of balls hitting the court makes me grin.

Cake and I grab balls and start to shoot.

I spot Coach Demer, our middle school basketball coach. He's one of the instructors. He looks much older than the rest of them. I purposely walk by, hoping to get his attention.

"Hey, Coach," I say. "How are you?"

He ignores me as he walks past. Maybe he didn't hear. Hopefully, I can make a better impression this time around. I feel an unpleasant buzz in my neck.

Another instructor spots me and points to my shirt.

"All campers have to wear the Hoop Con T-shirt or jersey."

"Oh," I say, realizing everyone is wearing the gear we got in our bags.

I ask if they have a smaller shirt.

"Mine's XL," I say.

"We don't have any extra," he says in a hurry. "Limited supply. People are copping them already online."

Cake's already removing his shirt. He has no shame. He always likes to tell people he has handles. He'll dribble the ball, grab his stomach, jiggle it, and laugh. I wish I had that self-esteem.

I head into the bathroom. I hate changing with people around me.

I have a condition called pectus excavatum. It's a genetic deformity where my chest looks sunken because the sternum and rib cage are abnormally shaped. The Moore brothers call me the Dent.

I would wear two shirts during PE so I didn't have to show anyone. During one class, we had to play shirts and skins during basketball. Justin started calling me Pigeon and Larry Birdchest. That didn't prevent me from drilling a three and flapping my hands in his direction. I felt confident until I observed Reena laughing and giggling in my direction. I looked for my shirt but someone had stolen it, so I hid under the bleacher clutching my arms around my body. At least Cake had an extra hoodie in his locker. It was hard to show my face in school the rest of the week without Justin tossing bread crumbs at me.

Luckily, only a few other kids are there, so I change quickly in a stall.

The jersey is too big, so I twist and roll the sleeves into knots. I look like I'm wearing Aron's actual uniform.

I get back into the room as Cake captures it in his camera. The campers and instructors all gather at one of the half-courts. I notice all the film people around capturing everything. Cake and I head over to the group. I keep biting my lip.

The drills are no joke. They divide us into groups of eight. Cake is teamed with Payton's group. I'm paired with ET and One-Up.

They set stations for shooting fundamentals, dribbling skills, passing and catching, perimeter skills, post skills, rebounding, and defense. We do some full-court group work (passing, catching, dribbling, fast-break tennis balls, and weaving around chairs).

In one shooting drill, they even use a broom to block us. I'm huffing and puffing as the sneakers screech across the wooden floor, my hands aching.

Across from us, Payton makes Cake and his group all look like elementary schoolkids as he dribbles around them.

In one drill where we have to dribble two balls, I lose the grip on one of them, causing it to knock off my knee. A cameraman captures it all and shakes his head at me pitifully while walking away to another group. I look at the ground feeling a cold sweat.

Thankfully, the morning session ends. Lunch will be served. Our stomachs growl as we sit on the bleachers perspiring. I swig my water bottle and hear an uproar. A few confused instructors start talking into a walkie-talkie. They seem baffled. They run toward the door a moment later, like there's an emergency outside. Cake and I spring up and start running that way too. One of the kids runs out the door panting in excitement.

"He's here!" he says. "Aron's here."

POSTERIZED

Like Black Friday shoppers, everyone runs toward the doors. Security does its best to keep people away. However, everyone busts outside to see Aron emerge from his new Maybach Exelero, which we heard wasn't even out to the public. It's the most expensive car in the world. He's rocking brand-new low-top Sky Hardaways. I've never seen those before.

Cake and I look at each other. No way.

He is blinged out in a giant diamond necklace and earring. People run up to him, trying to snap photos and videos. He obliges even as security tries to whisk them away. He's way taller in person, and his hair is cropped short. He's cut off his famous braids for a low-top fade. He rocks his own Sky Hardaway gear.

The crazy thing is Aron's only twenty years old. We've been following him since high school. Not since LeBron or Wemby was there a player this hyped.

He's a trampoline, blending power and acrobatic insanity. He can make a monthly calendar with all the people he posterizes. He's way bigger and taller. He also has handles that make you blink twice and rewatch three times because you're like, how did he do that? Now he's steps away, the actual human flesh and being.

The camera crew grabs every frame like it's rehearsed from a script. Cake and I try to greet Aron. Our pulses are racing. Security tightens around him from all sides and pushes us away.

Someone shouts, "When are you gonna show us that new dunk?"

The voice comes from behind me.

Aron chuckles.

"Maybe later today after lunch. Y'all hungry?" he asks.

I swear he looks at me while saying this.

The instructors inform us we should report to the food court to eat. We walk over in droves. None of us have eaten. Aron's bought lunch for all of us. Cake and I walk with One-Up and Hesh.

"I'm starving. These drills are intense," Cake says, drained. "I got teamed up with Justin on the tennis ball drill, and he kept throwing it at my head. The instructor never saw it."

"Man, I can't wait until Justin gets his due," I mention as we see a buffet spread out with pizza, chips, salad, scones, a taco bar, fruit, and a carving station when we get through the doors. All of us look at one another.

"There's more food here than at an Indian wedding," I joke.

"My uncle's wedding had more than this," One-Up chimes in, puffing his chest out. "He had ten courses, and Wolfgang Puck catered it."

As I said, the guy always has to one-up whatever you say.

We roll our eyes as we grab plates and utensils and get in the crowded line.

I grab a slice of pizza, chips, and a chocolate cookie. Cake samples everything.

We head to our seats. I can't believe I'm eating this cuisine instead of the regular stale nuggets and raw veggies. Mom used to make me bologna sandwiches. She barely has time these days.

One-Up, ET, and Hesh sit with us.

We scan around for Aron. We see instructors and coaches. Aron is out of sight.

"Raam, isn't lunch the time when you stare at Reena?" Cake says, busting my chops.

I scowl at him as he starts laughing.

Both her cousins glare at me, waiting to tear my insides out.

"What do you mean?" Hesh erupts.

"Nothing. Cake's playing," I say.

I stare dead-eyed at him.

"Right, Cake?"

I kick him under the table to make sure he gets the point. He winces.

"Yeah, uh, of course," he says meekly. "Only joking."

This barely helps, but their anger subsides as they continue to eat.

I scowl at Cake again. He shrugs.

"Better not try anything, Raam," Hesh says menacingly. "That's my cousin, bro."

"Yeah, don't even think about it, bro," One-Up one-ups.

Think about what? I want to ask. But I let it go. All I think about is getting back on the court.

A minute later, we all burp and try not to nap from our food comas. Cake feigns collapsing on the bench. We drag ourselves back to the courts. Our lethargy dissipates when we see Aron dunking over a set of barstools like it's an everyday thing ordinary people do.

Drills commence. I start individual dribbling drills with the chair. All groups continue to rotate. I look to see if Aron is around. I don't see him.

I'm struggling with the drill. My ballhandling has been a bit off today. Prolly nerves. I can't grip the ball properly.

Our instructor, this college kid named Gordon who has a soul patch, keeps telling me to keep my knees bent and head up. It's not helping.

Gordon whistles.

Thankfully, we are told to meet near the main court a few minutes later. We head over.

The crowd is much larger now. It's not campers, instructors, and cameramen anymore. There is the news and other press, and we all gather around the court.

We are all seated around the half-court. All four corners are packed with us kids sitting down, crowds of us awaiting, anticipating, and unable to relax. Everyone is restless. Even though we've been balling for hours, we wait to see Aron.

Cake finds me. He has his camera and monopod out.

"Yo, I heard he's dropping his new dunk today."

"I'm gonna audition for his new commercial tomorrow," One-Up says. "My uncle knows his agent's brother."

We all laugh.

The music lowers, and the DJ starts playing a beat.

The lights in the gym dim. The instructors even put up fake smoke and strobe lights. Another instructor named Rich gets on a mic. He's the size of Kevin Hart, and he belongs to Aron's crew. I even think he went to high school with him. He acts like his hype man.

"Introducing last year's MVP and your starting forward from the University of Illinois . . . Aron 'Sky' Hardaway."

The crowd goes bonkers, hollering, cheering, and clapping.

Aron comes out and high-fives the kids on the sideline. We are sitting just a little away. The crowd is crazy loud. Hundreds of us see our hero. Cameras click, mobile phones snap. Crazy that he's rocking another new pair of Sky Hardaways. I have never seen these before. They are low-cut and clear like a splash painting. That's three new kicks so far today. He also wears a dope hoodie with his Aron brand on it. I need one of those too.

He grabs a microphone and a ball.

The music dips. Aron stands near the top of the key. All of us are wild'n out. The best player in the game is right there in front of us.

He taps the mic. We feel the vibration of the feedback.

"Camps like this are where we find passion and love for the sport. Enjoy yourself, challenge yourself, and work together as a group. Something I want to stress is to help each other out and learn from each other."

He stops and drinks some water. We listen intently.

"Go out, enjoy yourselves, compete hard, and thank your parents. My mom worked at a bank for twenty years, and my dad worked on the assembly line, putting together surveillance cameras every day. They never complained. They did whatever they could to ensure I had enough to get by. So thank your parents and always focus on the work. 'Cause you can't win without the work. Enjoy yourselves. Play the game. I'll be stopping by all the stations to watch."

After he finishes, we all applaud and break up into new

groups. I'm selected into Coach Demer's group along with Payton. We see Aron with a whistle around his neck walking around. He's on the other side of the gym. I hope he stops by our area.

Coach Demer has us doing one-on-one drills. Around our half-court are two cones set up by the baseline.

"This is a corner finishing drill. I'll have a line of players line up here."

He points to an area near the basket.

"And I'll have another group line up here," he says, pointing underneath the opposite side of the basket from where I stand.

He explains one side will play defense while the other will play offense and try to score. We must run around the cone and try to score or defend the basket.

"Run around the cone as fast as you can. Change direction and score. Attacking and finishing," Coach Demer explains. "The other runs around and tries to stop him. No malicious fouls. Play good D. All right, let's go."

I visualize this will be the type of situation I'll be in next year when I make the team.

I realize I'm teamed up with Payton. We see Payton's dad

with the film crew and a dozen other production people capturing everything in every area. They got more coverage than an
All-Star Game.

I tie my shorts and my laces. I nod at Payton. He scoffs.

"You have to be kidding me," he says, sizing me up.

He towers over me.

"You don't fool me," I say, smacking the ball with my palm.

Coach Demer blows the whistle.

"Go."

My sneakers screech loud as I explode, ball in hand around
the corner. I can see Payton out of the corner of my eye. He's six
inches taller than me, so I must move my legs quicker and stay
low to the ground. As we turn, I can see Payton approaching me
like a tiger, and I know I can shoot, get my shot stuffed, or take
it to the hold.

I pump-fake and take my shot. The worst outcome is that he
blocks it.

I pretend to heave a shot, and Payton comes flying at me like
a jumbo jet. I duck. I don't think he realizes how short I am.
He's well past me, and I launch.

Swish Family Robinson!

The ball falls through—the kids on the sideline gasp. Payton walks past me.

"Lucky shot," he says.

I can't help but smile. I look around to see if Aron saw it. He missed it.

Payton glowers at me. He gets the ball this time, and I have to play defense. I know his moves, so I know he will Eurostep to the basket with his left hand. He takes me to the rack, but I keep up with his action and distract him enough to miss the shot. I try to grab the rebound, but he shoves me to the ground. He catches the ball, and I jump back up and hack him hard over the face. I'm steaming.

Coach blows the whistle. His face is red.

"This is a drill. Not some UFC match. You two need to calm down."

Aron watches from the bleachers. He and Coach nod and signal at each other.

"I have a better idea," Coach Demer says. "Why don't you two settle this with a one-on-one game?"

"Sounds good to me," I say, rubbing my hands together.

"I'm about to teach you a lesson, Mugsy," Payton says, glaring.

Our commotion draws the attention of other campers, especially when Aron walks toward the sideline to get a closer look.

Rich, the guy who introduced Aron, grabs a mic.

"Looks like we got a little competition at Hoop Con," Rich says, offering play-by-play. "The great Payton Newman squaring off against . . ."

He pauses and looks around.

"Raam Patel!" someone shouts. It's Cake. Of course, it's Cake.

Aron walks by and sits near us though other games are going on. Payton's dad sits next to him in the bleachers. They have the entire camera crew focused on our game.

The instructors bring us to half-court to explain the rules.

Coach Demer cracks a joke at Gordon.

"This is gonna be rough," he says.

Great, Demer doesn't have faith in me.

But that's fine. I'll prove it again. I thrive under pressure.

"Let's get this started," Coach Demer says.

Payton snickers loudly. This is a joke for him, not for me.

I glance at Aron. He's laughing and pointing with Payton's dad.

Coach Demer blows the whistle.

"Oh!" Rich adds color commentary like a wrestling promoter.

The crowd also stirs.

"Let's go," Payton says.

"Going to 5, Chi-Town rules," Coach Demer says. "Make it, take it."

Payton takes a simple three-pointer. Nothing but net.

"My ball."

The DJ starts the music now, and the crowd starts hollering.

I look over to Cake, and he's recording all of it. Everyone is capturing this. People are standing, hands over their heads, arms crossed, stretched out, smiling and laughing. And of all people, I notice Mom in the stands. She must be here early.

The instructors also watch from their stations. They all want to be entertained.

My heart starts pumping.

Payton takes the ball and checks it for me. I fling it back to him. He starts to dribble and tosses the ball at my head. It smacks me and bounces back to him. I tune out for a second. People in the crowd laugh. Cheap move. I ignore it.

I clap my hands angrily. I check the ball back to him harder.

"Oh, Too Short, getting a little feisty," he says.

I grab and pull the end of my shorts and spread my hands. A flood of manic energy passes through me. I'm boiling. I have to remember I know all his moves. Payton has trouble with his weak hand; no matter how well he handles the rock, most of it is smoke and mirrors. I need to nag him like a gnat. He hates that, and his temper gets in his way. I'm going to annoy him.

And that's what I do. Stick to him like superglue. I attack and don't let go. He tries to punk me. I'm not falling for it. I keep on him until he picks up his dribble. He tries to use his height. I keep my hands up and jump like a madman. I poke the ball from his grip. It goes out of bounds. The vein in Payton's neck is visible. He isn't happy. I retrieve the ball.

I'm feeling stoked and want to join in on the trash talk.

"I'm going to shoot it right in your face again," I say.

All the kids around go, "Whoa!"

He laughs initially, but his smile turns into something more sinister, almost feral.

"I'm about to make you look stupid," Payton says, clenching his jaw.

He grabs another ball and bounces it hard off the floor, and it hits the backboard and comes back to him. He slaps it hard. I hope he doesn't look at my head as a ball.

"You might wanna lace those up," Payton says, tossing the ball away.

I realize one of my shoes is untied again.

I bend to tie them. Payton does the same, staring me down. I've seen him do this to opponents before. His eyes stare at you without a blink, peering into your soul. He pulls up his own socks to his knees. They are ugly.

I'm nervous. I take a deep breath. I'm facing the best player my age, and my favorite player of all time is watching us. The only way I can even challenge Payton is not to back down.

Instead of checking the ball with him, I walk over and stuff the ball into his chest.

"Oh, getting spunky," Rich says. His narration pumps up the crowd.

Payton steps back. He looks at me briefly, almost snarling. He swings the ball over his face, wiping the look off it, and replaces it with a smile.

He starts to dribble right to left. I know he has skills. I need not be intimidated. Pretend he's just another kid I need to take candy from. I set my position. I'm a ninja, stealthy and quick. I take a jab. Nothing. He stops and takes a three. The ball rises high, comes halfway down the net, and then spins out.

"Oh no, Payton bricked it."

Payton's stunned for a quick second, so I grab the board.

"Uh-oh, little man, got the ball."

I take the ball back to the key.

"Take it to the rack," some kids yell.

I quickly dash back to the three-point line. I have to impress Aron.

Payton runs at me. I'm going to hit a three again. Same way. This time for the cameras. I stop and pump-fake again, but Payton doesn't fall for it this time. Now, I'm trapped again. I try to move, but his long arms are all over me like he's Doctor Octopus. I double-pump. I feel his eyes on me like I'm being hunted. I try pivoting and shooting it. He smacks the ball with the force of a volleyball being spiked. The ball sails far toward the other side of the gym. Some kids go to retrieve it.

When they come back, the ball is flattened. It's not the only thing that feels deflated.

"Wow, get a new ball, folks," Rich says, amazed. "I've never seen that before."

Someone tosses us another ball. I pass it back to Payton. My equilibrium is shot. My confidence cracks. He passes it back to me. This time I shoot the ball as soon as I can. I miss badly. Payton grabs the board.

He points at me as he dribbles the ball back and forth from left to right. Suppose he wants a staring contest. Fine. It's like a snake charmer, and suddenly, the ball disappears even as he pretends to dribble. And he takes off. As I turn around, I see the ball, and Payton grabs it, goes through his legs, and double-pumps and reverse dunks it. By the time he lands, the crowd goes bonkers. I'm stunned. Payton rouses up the crowd, poses for the cameras, and high-fives all the kids around him.

"Dang," is all Rich can say. "Kid, you've been baptized."

Someone throws me the ball back. Payton checks it. Smiles. He's back in his comfort zone.

"Remember this. This will be your school lesson for the year."

I toss the ball back. Before I can even try to guard him, he shoots. The ball hits nothing, not even the net.

"That's 3–0, kid," Rich says.

Payton checks the ball back to me. As soon as I catch it, I slow roll it back to him.

Cake films everything from the sidelines.

I give him more space. I'm not going to fall for that trick again. This time, Payton slows the ball down deliberately. He wants to set me up for something. He paces and prowls with the ball. I know he's going to take a jumper.

He accelerates, and I lean in. My feet are like skates, and I lose my balance as Payton steps back and puts the ball between his ankles. I fall right on my butt. Payton steps back and fires a jumper. Drills it. I'm still on the ground.

I can hear the laughs.

"Payton just made that boy touch the earth," Rich says. "Dude, your ankles aren't broken, are they?"

I get up and brush myself off. I look over at the crowd and see Aron laughing. Probably at me.

"Game point, folks," Rich says.

"You're out of your league," Payton says. "'Bout to send you back to elementary school."

He takes the ball and goes at me full force. He lifts off. I try to get in his way to take charge. He jumps over me from the free-throw line, and his feet curl like Jordan. I can feel the force over me like a jet. The momentum makes me lose my balance again, and I fall back and see this giant shadow hover and come down.

I'm still on my back watching.

"OMG, that's over. Savage," Rich says. "The gravity got sucked out of here."

The crowd rushes, cell phones on, toward Payton as he basks in the glow of the cameras. I look around and see Aron shaking his head in shame. He doesn't even look at me.

All these kids rush past me. No one helps me up. I can see other kids filming me. I am still dazed and confused. It feels like I got hammered. My head feels dizzy and numb.

"Bro, hang that in the Louvre," Dustin shouts.

"You got posterized," Justin says with his phone in my face.

There's this swarm of people. My head feels this heat, and I only want to run away.

"You still have your soul?" One-Up says to me.

I'm shaking and feel something creep on my face.

My chest tightens.

I look around and see my mom stunned in the stands. Her hand over her mouth. Some of the campers follow me with their phones. I pull myself up. My legs feel weak.

I bolt out of the building as fast as I can. I don't want to look back.

PARENT TRAP

I sprint out of the ballroom, covering my ears. I feel like my insides have been dipped into hot oil. I nearly run into a camera guy. I need to get away from everyone. Mom has parked, so I have to find our minivan in the parking garage.

Outside, Hoop Con is still going strong. I'm sure they heard about Payton posterizing me or Aron's reaction when he saw me play. All these thoughts pound in my brain. I want to find a place to hide. I run through the trade show with its skylights beaming right on me, through atriums and meeting rooms, and finally stop in a loading dock area with forklifts and large trucks moving giant boxes and equipment.

I wish I could pull my jersey over my face and avoid anyone looking at me, but they would see my bird chest. My heart hammers inside me, and I know my eyes are watery. No way I can let anyone see me like this. A loud honk stops me in my tracks. I look and see the high-beam lights of a Mack Truck. I freeze. The driver yells something, but it feels muted and distant. I keep running and finally find the parking garage.

I search exhaustively for minutes for Mom's van. All these white minivans look alike. Finally, I find ours parked in the back with its OM bumper sticker and Florida Gators license plate.

I tug at the door. It's locked, and I have no key. I smack the car with my fist. My legs feel rubbery, and my calves are aching. Eyes burn. My mind's dizzy, and I want to throw up. I crouch down by the tire, exhausted, ashamed, and embarrassed, even more than when I air-balled a three during the morning ball when Reena watched. I could pretend I got hacked. And no one had a phone to capture it all.

I hear the hum of traffic and the roar of a nearby lawn mower, and music booms from the convention center in the distance. The ugly tears stream down my cheek. I clench my eyes tighter.

A gentle hand touches my shoulder. It's Mom.

I open my eyes. They are sticky and wet, and I can feel snot. I wipe it all with my jersey.

I sure don't want Mom seeing me, let alone anyone, in this state.

"I was looking for you everywhere," she says, taking a napkin from her purse and trying to dab my face.

I push her hand away.

"I'm fine," I say. "Just want to go home."

My voice is a blubbering mess of uncontrolled tears.

"I saw you running."

"Mom, I don't want to talk about it. I want to go."

I get up and fidget with the door again. I feel my head heating up, and I want to break the whole car.

"Can you please open the door?" I ask, my voice breaking into a whimper.

"Yes, of course, sorry," she says, juggling through her purse.

She digs the key out and presses the unlock button. I hear the chirp and open the door.

I jump into the van and the back seat and lie down, hoping to hide from any onlookers.

Mom gets in the front and starts the car. She's staring at me in the rearview. When she turns on the car's engine, loud bhangra beats blare from the speakers. She quickly shuts it off.

We exit the parking garage, and the sky is pitch-dark, and the afternoon summer storm is pouring down on us in heavy beads of rain. The whole ride home, I don't say a word. It's pure silence. Mom keeps staring at me from the rearview, not letting me out of her sight as the wipers wave back and forth. My body feels numb.

I bolt out and run through the door while she parks the car in the driveway. I dart toward my room. Only I notice Dad and his camera equipment are blocking my path.

Dad looks haggard and soaked like he's been driving through the rain for hours. He's removed his fedora, his go-to hat. Underneath, his hair is graying, thinning, and wet. He always combs it back, and I know he gets sensitive when Mom rubs it. The stubble on his face glints in the light. He spots me from the doorway. He's adjusting a tripod. Around him are camera filters, lenses, white boxes, and various lights.

"What's up, kiddo?" he says, cracking a smile.

He grabs a samosa from a container and pops it into his mouth.

I'm still processing my embarrassment.

77

The alarm chirps, the garage door cracks open, and Mom enters. She is sopping wet. She closes an umbrella.

She looks surprised to see Dad.

"Oh, I didn't think you were coming till tomorrow," she says.

"Hello to you as well," he says.

"How did the property work out?"

"Too expensive," he says. "I did come up with an idea on my drive back. I meant to talk to you about it."

Mom steps back. She sighs. She looks at the equipment like they are spilled LEGO® bricks.

"What?" he asks.

I've seen this scene before between them.

"Nothing," she says. "Go ahead."

"Never mind," he says. His smile is gone, and now he bites his teeth hard.

"I don't want to bother you with a half-baked thought," he says.

"I didn't say anything," she says.

I remember this happened a few weeks ago and countless times before that.

Mom would ask for something like, say, a cup of coffee. Dad

would halfway respond he was on his way to a meeting, stop, hesitate, and retrieve the coffee.

Dad would give it to her, and Mom would ask if he put in creamer.

"No, it's just black," he would say. "I did what you asked."

"No, you half-baked it," she says. "I can get it myself."

She would get up, and Dad would roll his eyes and leave.

It was frustrating because these were my parents, and they would act like someone my age.

Mom takes a breath and wipes off the rain with a towel.

"Tell me," she asks.

"Well, this hotel industry world doesn't make me happy," he says. "I'm thinking about starting the creative agency we talked about."

I can see Mom's demeanor tense up.

"Okay," she says.

Dad cranes his neck and cracks it.

"You're making a decent salary now," she says.

"I don't want to work for someone else," he says. "We can work together again."

"No, I don't want to return to where we were," she says. "It's impossible to work with you, and I'm happy with my academy."

Dad turns pale and starts biting his nails.

"It's not about money," he says. "It's about being happy."

"I wasn't happy working with you," she says.

"Happy working with me or happy being with me?"

"Naresh, don't twist my words," Mom says. "Can we discuss all this later?"

"Why not now?"

Mom points to me. I'm staring at all this, numb.

"Your son had a rough day."

Dad looks at me like it's the first time he realizes I'm in the room.

"What happened? Did you spell something wrong?" he asks sarcastically.

"No," I say as I show him the logo on the shirt. He recognizes the name finally.

"So you went to Hoop Con?" he asks. "We decided you were going to spelling bee camp."

"You decided," Mom says. "This wasn't a group decision."

Dad drops the tripod accidentally, and it lands with a thud, causing other equipment to fall, including a big lens that cracks on the ground. Dad picks it up.

"Don't worry, I paid for the camp," she says.

"What does that mean?"

"Just because you won't pay for something doesn't mean I can't."

Dad rolls his eyes. He looks at the broken lens. Mom clenches her teeth.

"Great, now that's also money down the drain," he says.

I wanted to bring up the fact that I sold the card, had my own money, and could pay Mom back. But I feel my body go lame, and I go silent.

"When did I even say that?" he says. "I want him to think about other things than basketball."

"Well, you should ask him what happened today," she says, staring at me.

I look at her, mouth ajar. This is what happens when they argue. I get thrown into the middle of their dysfunction. Sometimes I prefer them to do their own thing.

I turn around and leave.

"What happened?" Dad asks me.

I pretend not to hear him.

I bang my door open with such force the mini-hoop rim on the side ends up putting a dent into the drywall and bends the rim into an oval. I don't care. I slam the door shut and lock it.

I still hear Payton laughing, Justin and Dustin mocking, and Aron scoffing at me, and all I want to do is tune it all out. I notice Aron's posters on the wall. I can't stand to look at them. I want to trash the whole place like rockers do to hotel suites, but this is my room, and I'll have to do the housekeeping.

I leave everything as is and collapse on my bed from sheer exhaustion. I close my eyes tightly, hoping to wake up from this nightmare. This could be a parallel multiverse from a Marvel movie.

I pull my bed cover over my head and coil my body into a fetal position. I want to message Trina but realize I left my phone outside. There's a light knock on my door.

I ignore it. I know it's Mom.

She knocks again a little louder.

"Raam raja, are you okay?" Mom asks. Her voice is concerned. She's constantly worrying about me.

"I'm fine," I say. I don't want to explain anything right now.

"You know something like this happened to me when I was your age," she begins.

"Mom, I don't want to hear it," I say. "Can you leave me alone?"

"Okay, I need to stop by the studio and pick up some waiver forms," she says. "I should be back in thirty minutes. Your dad left already."

I put my face back into the pillow.

"Whatever."

"I left some food for you by the door," she says. I hear her footsteps retreat.

I linger for a few minutes. The fragrant smell of fried food wafts under the door and into my room—filling up my nose. I realize I haven't eaten since lunch. Funny how hungry you can get when you've been clowned in front of an entire gym.

I open the door to find a plate of warm chicken samosas and mint chutney. I gobble them all and leave the plate by the door like I'm a prisoner.

PUT ON SKATES

I leave my room to go to the bathroom. Loud music blares from the family room. Mom's in front of the television and practicing her choreography by watching Bollywood musical numbers. She's sweating. She pauses the video when she sees me. She tilts her head, smiling.

"Look who's emerged from his cocoon," she says jokingly.

I'm still numb and don't know what to say.

"I'm going to the bathroom," I point out.

"Wonderful. Want to see my new routine? It's a little Madhuri and a little Deepika."

"No, I'm okay."

"You know I got moves like Beyoncé." She winks.

Her playfulness is annoying.

"I don't want to know."

"You might want to know your phone has been buzzing non-stop since I got home," she alerts me.

She points to the phone on the counter.

"It's been going off for at least thirty minutes," she says, brow furrowing.

It dings again as I pick it up.

I glance down. It's an endless scroll of missed calls, text messages, and notifications.

Mom and Dad reluctantly let me get a phone. Only after I badgered them for months and guilt-tripped them about the safety angle did they allow me to have one. Cake had one too, and he helped by offering my parents a solid argument for teaching me personal responsibility. Dad rolled his eyes and gave in. He joked that Cake could sell salt to a slug.

I was only allowed a certain amount of screen time. I had Instagram, Twitter, and YouTube to watch highlights, comment on sneaker releases, and follow Aron.

No one knew my number besides Cake, my parents and grandparents, and Trina, but I had twenty-eight missed calls and a long list of texts. Calls from area codes I'd never seen from 908 to 424.

The messages were random:

Yoooo Raaam, that's crazy.

Hope you are doing ok.

We pray for you and your family.

See what talking trash got you.

Yo, that video was savage.

Someone calls me. It's an unknown number but the same area code for Orlando. I pick up.

"Raam Patel got dunked on. HAHA."

The caller hangs up. But I recognize the voice. It's one of the Moore brothers. But I'm not sure where he got my number from. I call back, but it goes straight to voice mail.

"Who was that?" Mom asks.

"Some kid from school," I say.

"How did he get the number?"

"I don't know."

I check out my social media feeds. I scroll Instagram,

and the first video I see is posted from Payton's account.

It's a highlight of our one-on-one game, but it's cut up with high-end graphics and slick edits. It's cut to music, and I watch in horror repeatedly as I get dunked on. The caption reads:

You got put on skates and touched the earth.

Luckily, there aren't many views or comments. He just posted, though.

Mom asks me again. She walks up to me and puts her arm on my shoulder.

"What's going on, Raam?" she asks. "Everything okay?"

My mind starts racing, and Mom keeps bugging me.

"I'm fine. Can I have a little privacy? I'm twelve now."

I pull away. She's taken aback.

"Okay, young man. I'll give you space. But don't talk to me disrespectfully."

"Sorry. I have to go to the bathroom."

I quickly retreat. I use the restroom, scroll around, and see the video appearing on different platforms.

After I'm done, I text Trina.

ME: **I got totally embarrassed by Payton Newman at Hoop Con.**

TRINA: **No way. Don't worry about it. Happens to all of us.**

ME: **Video is already up.**

TRINA: **Those get posted all the time. Don't worry. Attention spans are short. No one will think about it. It's in your head.**

ME: **ok. Thanks, hope you're right.**

TRINA: **I'm always right . . .**

When I get back to my room, I crash on the bed. My phone battery has dwindled, and the screen shuts down. I'm too tired to charge it. Somehow, I drift asleep, visions of getting dunked on hover over me, and the voices of everyone laughing echo in my head . . .

I wake up with the sun sending harsh angles off my face. My phone battery is drained. Good, I don't want to start the day being connected. I hear noise from outside. I am still in my uniform from yesterday, soaked in sweat. Yesterday's nightmare comes rushing back like a waterfall. It was all real. I plug my phone in, realizing I must go to Hoop Con again today.

As soon as the screen loads up, I am bombarded by an end-less list of notifications, missed calls, and text messages. Like ten times what I got last night. I notice Cake and Trina called me several times and texted.

TRINA: **OMG. RU OK? Call me.**

CAKE: **DUDE!**

I first check Twitter. Payton's tweets have exploded. He has over 50,000 likes, and it's been retweeted 10,000 times. I switch to YouTube, and the video is the first in my feed.

Over 100,000 views since it got posted last night. There are 3,000 comments and they're nasty and full of emojis:

His life ended at 11 years old. Tragic.

That kid sees this in his nightmares before he wakes up 10 years later.

That kid must be SO embarrassed watching this.

There should be a meme for that kid's reaction.

I close my phone and head outside.

Mom's in the kitchen clutching a mug and drinking her chai. She looks at me and smiles.

"Sleep okay?"

I'm panicking.

"Did you see all this?" I say, pointing to the phone. My breathing is sporadic, and it feels like I'm having a panic attack. "I've gone viral. The video from Hoop Con was posted, and now everyone knows who I am."

Mom takes a look at my phone and sees all the messages.

She puts her hand over her face.

"What is it?"

"These comments. They're brutal."

The phone buzzes. Mom picks up the call.

"Hello?" she says into the phone. "No, this is his mom. And no, he isn't commenting. Who is this? Well, how did you get this number?"

I hear a phone click.

She looks at me.

"Don't worry about it. It will wash over. Chul, get ready for Hoop Con. We're running late."

I look at her dumbfounded. Is she kidding?

Mom tries to pour me some cereal.

"I don't think you should overthink this. You're probably hungry."

I look at her incredulously as if she inhabits a different planet.

I don't know how to react.

"I'm not going," I say, completely shocked.

"Um, yes, you are," Mom says. "I've already paid the bill. This wasn't cheap, Raam. That's a week pass. I have to teach extra lessons on top of my classes."

"There is no way I'm showing my face outside this house ever again."

"I'm serious; you are going. There are no return policies."

"I'm the number one stooge," I say angrily. "Why put me through this humiliation? Didn't you do enough?"

I'm getting pissed. It's 7:45, and I want to run away as fast as possible and move to some remote rainforest.

"Fine," Mom says. "But you are going to spelling bee camp. You're at least going to learn something."

I put my head down on the table. I relent.

Fine. At least they won't have a clue what happened. None of them care much for basketball.

#RAAMING

Mom drops me off in front of the temple.

I'm late. Even though it's not officially school, Nupur Auntie has strict rules regarding truancy.

When I get to the classroom, all the kids break down SAT words' origins and roots.

I try to slip in, but Auntie spots me through her bifocals.

The kids all stare at me.

"Raam, we were talking about how the word *late* originates from Middle English and German."

"Sorry, Auntie," I say. "It's been a rough morning."

She offers me a nod of sympathy.

"It's okay. I didn't think you were coming anymore after your mom messaged me yesterday," she says. "I'm surprised to see you."

A few laughs erupt from some of the other kids.

I spot Anup's younger brother, Sandeep. He's still in elementary school but even more annoying than One-Up.

I give him the evil eye, and he turns away.

"We're going to start our mock bee after this break. Get some exercise or a drink and be back in fifteen minutes," Nupur Auntie says.

I get up and walk out to the hallway to get a drink from the fountain. Sandeep and a group of other kids are hanging out nearby.

"Saw him on *SportsCenter*'s Not Top 10 this morning," he says loud enough so I can overhear. "That's harsh. Worse than missing the first word in a spelling bee."

"I wonder if he can spell *posterize*," someone says. I hear loud laughter.

I scratch my throat, making my presence known, and they scamper away.

Ganesh's statue stares at me, and I try to practice a breathing exercise.

When we get back, we are given construction paper and string. We make our placards like they wear in real bees.

If there were a Heisman Trophy, it would go to Puja Gohill. She's the top speller in the class and made it to DC last year. This year she's easily a finalist.

She's got the dedication; I'll tell you that. She's an upcoming sixth grader with braces. These kids hit the dictionary like it's lifting weights or practicing jumpers in the gym.

Some might not consider spelling a sport, but it's equally competitive, especially with this group.

I had my spelling bee phase a few years ago. But my parents were obsessed with it, and Dad became way too competitive.

I gave up after tripping on the word *logorrhea* in fifth grade. Reena won the bee that year.

Now, I am back by force.

All of us sit at our desks. Some kids bring the entire dictionary, which weighs more than they do. Some bring tablets.

Auntie starts the bee. She taps her cards on her desk. She tasks Sandeep with asking us to spell. I'm the first to go. He asks me to spell *vivisepulture*.

"What is the definition, please?"

"The practice of burying someone alive."

"What is the root?"

"Latin."

"What is the part of speech?"

"Noun."

"Can I get it in a sentence?"

"Payton Newman practiced the *vivisepulture* when he dunked on Raam at Hoop Con."

Everyone starts to crack up and stare at me.

I turn red.

"You know, I can send you back to your point of origin," I say, pounding my fist.

"That's enough from both of you," Auntie sneers as she gets up and slaps her cards loudly on her desk. "Raam, we don't threaten classmates with violence."

She points to a photo of Mahatma Gandhi with a walking stick.

"Sandeep, we do not make jokes like that."

"Sorry, Auntie," he says.

"Raam, I did see that video in our aunties' WhatsApp group. I understand how you might feel," she says.

Really? I want to ask. She has no clue.

"Can I spell the word?"

"Yes, go ahead."

I spell it correctly.

I glower at Sandeep. He sinks lower in his seat.

Spelling bees might not be my court, but I will not be the butt of anyone's joke.

I don't make it to the next round.

I miss the word *piquant*.

I can't believe the incident reached all the way here. There's no place to go now. I bury my nose in a dictionary for the rest of the class and avoid everyone's gaze.

Mom picks me up. We don't say anything on the way home. She knows I won't go to another class. At least Dad isn't there. He's in Georgia for another shoot.

I check my phone. Things have gone from bad to worse.

I search my Twitter handle, and there are thousands of replies and messages. I don't even know how they found me. I see Cake's account and the post. He's tagged me.

It's a video with the simple caption:

savage

The video starts to play and already has 500,000 views and Cake's watermark.

He uses the same on-screen graphics and logos we use for our trick videos and makes a highlight clip of me getting posterized with the hashtag #raaming.

There are already 150,000 likes and 4,000 comments.

I quickly scroll some of the feed to get a sampling.

It's littered with emojis and movie GIFs and LOLs.

I watch the clips. I look awful, entirely like a moron. I'm stunned. I want to text Cake, but what's the point?

And Aron retweeted him too. Along with Payton. Everything snowballs.

It's now become more extensive than I thought.

I check YouTube again and sure enough, a different video of the moment is there.

It's titled: **PAYTON TAKING DUDE'S SOUL.**

Over a million views in three hours.

I ask Mom if she has TikTok.

"Um, yes," she says, slightly embarrassed. "I use it to check Bollywood dance trends. It's what all the kids are using."

"I'm not judging you now," I say. "Tell me if you see anything."

She puts her hand over her face.

"What is it?"

I look. Dread.

The first hashtag trending is #raaming.

Every video is me getting posterized at every angle or tripping on my butt.

I clutch my stomach in pain. I want to hide under my bed and never come out.

BALL HOG

I need fresh air. I need to breathe. I wander outside to the porch. There's only one place at home where I feel the most relaxed. Yes, the court is my oasis, but not sure that's the case anymore.

In our backyard screened porch, weeds start to grow along the cracks in the concrete. We have a dining table with chairs caked with dust and rust and a wooden swing called a jhula covered in cobwebs. Mom imported it from India from Apple Dada's house. This was the swing she sat on when she was a little girl and the one my grandfather would rock back and forth on when he would tell me stories of the Mahabharata and Ramayana and cut me apples. When Dada passed away last year, Mom brought the swing from India after Bha sold the house and moved in with Sanjeev Mama, Mom's brother.

I have been to India only twice. Once when I was three, the other time was in fourth grade.

I rip down the webs and sit in the swing with its dark wood carvings and Indian lettering. I like to nap in it with a pillow or simply glide back and forth and close my eyes. And right now, that's what I want to do. I rock back and forth, crossing my ankles.

I could see the red spectrum go orange and the sun bright. I can feel the warm air envelop me.

My Zen moments get interrupted by Cake yelling across the golf course. He's the last person I want to see, especially after tagging me in his video.

"Where did you go?" Cake asks, wearing his new Aron jersey. "You disappeared yesterday. I called and texted. You won't believe it. Aron just retweeted me and reposted my video."

He walks through the screen door. He shows me his phone.

"I got owned," I remind him again. "I can't believe you posted that video and tagged me."

"I didn't post until other people did. I didn't know Aron would retweet mine."

"You have to take this down. I look like a chump."

"No way," Cake says. "I already have 45K more followers on Instagram, 75K on TikTok, and 25K on Twitter, including Aron and Payton."

His nostrils flair.

"So what?" I say, my voice beginning to crack. "All at my expense."

"Dude, you are taking this way too seriously."

"I've already become a hashtag," I say.

I rub my temple. It feels like a sharp knife keeps stabbing my brain.

"Bruh, you have gone viral."

"I got punked, and you are exploiting the moment."

How can he not understand this?

He looks at me strangely, turning his head.

"Man. Shouldn't have talked all that trash to Payton," he says.

I crack my knuckles hard.

"It was all in good fun," I respond. "And you're supposed to defend me. I thought you were my best friend."

"I am," he responds meekly.

"Okay, so take it down," I demand.

"No one's going to care," he says.

He's getting me more upset with his wishy-washy comments.

"I care," I say.

"No," he says finally. "This is my big break."

I grab his phone from his grip and frantically try to unlock it.

"Give it back, man," he says as I try to play keep-away.

Finally, I get the passcode. It's Aron's birthday.

"I'm deleting it," I say.

He grabs it. I push him back. My blood is boiling. He returns the favor, and the phone falls to the ground—the screen cracks into tiny spiderwebs.

He clutches it with a look of horror on his face. Tears begin to well up.

I don't feel bad, though. He deserves it.

"I want an apology," I demand.

"For what?" he says. "You broke my phone."

He grimaces.

"You ruined my life."

"You did that yourself."

I take a step back and sit down on the swing. This is all too much.

Suddenly, I hear the sliding glass door open. Mom pops her head out, looking concerned.

"Boys, is everything okay?" she asks. "I heard some shouting."

"Yes, we are fine," I say as casually as I can.

"All good, Auntie," Cake says, faking a smile.

"Glad to hear," Mom responds.

Mom smiles. Her face twitches. She turns back into the house.

I'm so furious. I want to go for the jugular.

"If you don't take it down, I don't want to be your teammate in Y-Ball," I say.

"Good, I don't, either," Cake responds. "No one wants to be your teammate. There's a reason you didn't make the team last year. You're a selfish ball hog. You deserve what Payton did to you."

Ouch. That hurt more.

He throws a tote bag in my direction.

"That's the crap you left when you ran out of the gym," he says, turning away. All I hear is a metal bang from the screen door. I don't say anything. I've gone numb.

Best friend, eh?

My chest feels tied to an iron ball and chain that's cast out to sea. I retake a seat on the swing to recover. Cake and I haven't argued like this since I accidentally asked Sheila Kalidas's mom, Kokila Auntie, if she got the bracelet Cake had given her. I didn't have my glasses on then, and I thought it was Sheila from a distance. It wasn't. It was Kokila Auntie.

That didn't go too well when she interrogated me with a million questions. I tried to cover it up. I failed miserably. I ruined Cake's one-week relationship with Sheila, and she ended up going to private school. He didn't talk to me for a month. And Kokila Auntie marked Cake as a young man you should keep away from your daughters.

This felt different. I owned up to my mistake. He denied it. And now my humiliation is increasing his views and follower count.

I grab the tote bag and head back inside, slamming the screen door.

TEMPLE OF DOOM

I lie low for the next few days. Mom leaves for the other bigger Hindu temple to train classes because the dance studio is getting fumigated for a wasp infestation. Dad's at Vipul Uncle's hotel getting drone footage of the new construction, and I'm hungry.

It's still 95-plus outside, and I'm still living life as a hermit, avoiding human contact in every way possible.

Mom even asked me to go to Publix, but the thought of a Pub Sub couldn't tempt me to leave for fear of being recognized.

I need something cold and sweet to eat with the mind-numbing heat. It's Popsicle season, and I know we have a box of Flintstone Push-Ups waiting to be digested. We have a fridge in the garage that Mom uses to store frozen food and house all her spices and mango aamras.

My paternal grandparents have a mango tree that produces way too much fruit, and my grandmother gives my mom containers full of aamras we don't know what to do with. I can't drink mango anymore because I've consumed it in every possible form from liquid to pickle to ice cream. I need my orange sherbet push-up.

I weave through the laundry room into the humid garage. It's always a mess. My dad loves accumulating stuff. He's a pack rat. He doesn't throw anything away, and I can barely ever find anything. Dad always plans on cleaning it out for our neighborhood's annual garage sale. Never happens. The collection just grows. I now realize where my stockpiling tendencies come from.

I pass the cleaning supplies, garbage, and recycling bins and walk past Christmas and Halloween decorations stuffed in clear containers and luggage piled high.

In one corner are Dad's boxes. Mom tried to get rid of them one time, and Dad threw a conniption. I have to navigate through this mess to get to the fridge.

I wind myself through and crack open the freezer. The wisp of cold feels cathartic, and I can hear the crunch of the frost on the aamras packets. I find my push-ups. It's muggy here, and I rip off the wrapper and taste the sweet orange sugar that's already melting.

Nearby I notice the tape holding some of Dad's boxes has peeled off the flaps, exposing their contents. Dad never lets me handle any of his stuff, whether collectibles or memorabilia. He would always be protective like they were exhibits in a vault that couldn't be touched.

I open a box up and am greeted by the large yellow eyes of a Dancing Jar Jar Binks toy from *The Phantom Menace*. For some reason, Dad has a box full of *Star Wars* action figures, vehicles, and cup holders from the prequel movies.

I spot Dad's old trophies in another box, including a few basketball ones. I know he played ball, but he doesn't talk about it, like most things, not with me anymore. Though he grew up in Orlando and is back home, he never felt comfortable. Even still.

Another nearby box also catches my attention. It's hidden behind the *Star Wars* box. It's labeled LA. This one is still shut. I'm surprised I haven't seen it before.

A thick layer of dust and cobwebs make me sneeze and cough.

I take a nearby screwdriver and slice the tape off. Inside is a cylindrical tube containing posters and a photo album.

I undo the rubber band and unroll one of the posters. It's for *Sati Shaves Her Head*, the name of the film my parents made long before I was born. They always talked about it like some old neighbor casually mentioned. They said I was too young to see it, and that was it whenever I asked.

The poster shows a photo of a bunch of teens around a barber chair. I notice Mom's and Dad's names in the credits. Mom is the director, and Dad is the producer.

I check out the photo book. It's a behind-the-scenes album, and I immediately see a photo of Amy Simone, the famous TV actress turned movie star. She's talking with Dad and Mom in several of the pictures. I can't honestly believe they know her.

The door from the house to the garage opens, and Dad pops his head in.

"What are you doing?" he asks suspiciously, like I'm a burglar opening up his stuff.

"What's all this?" I ask.

I show him the poster.

"Junk."

He stares intently at it.

"You didn't tell me you made a movie with Amy Simone."

"A long time ago, in a galaxy far, far away," he says dryly.

"That was her first movie, and we were the ones who cast her."

"That's awesome."

He puffs his chest out and nods his head.

I can tell he is proud of that feat by his tone.

"Anyway, that was the past."

"Why didn't you and Mom make another movie?" I ask.

If you made one movie, why wouldn't you make two?

"Not something I want to talk about."

I'm not surprised by that answer.

"Fine, but what about all these *Star Wars* toys?"

"Waste of money," he says, examining a Padmé action figure. "I thought I'd pay your college tuition with that. Now I'd be lucky to pay someone to haul it away. Anyway, put it all back. We have to go to the temple today."

"Why?" I ask suspiciously, like he wants to put me back in the spelling camp. Dad isn't religious and never goes to the temple. Mom, however, remains devout and will never miss a holiday or occasion to go.

"Today's the one-year anniversary when Apple Dada passed away," he says.

"Oh."

I take a step back. With all this craziness, I didn't realize it was June 30.

"Mom has a puja at the temple," he says. "We need to go."

A flood of memories comes rushing back, fueled with sadness and grief. Both Dad and I remain quiet for a moment. Fresh wounds never heal.

One year ago. I can recall it so vividly. I went to bed rewatching Aron's highlights, including his draft night from the year before. The Magic had selected Aron, who wore a burgundy plaid suit. He was the number-three pick like Michael Jordan. He performed better than anyone expected, winning Rookie of the Year. So there I was, dreaming of posterizing an opponent, when at 3 a.m., the call came. At first, I thought it was spam. My parents must have sent it to voice mail.

Then the phone rang again.

Dad had left his phone charging in the kitchen. I got up to see. It was, oddly, a North Carolina area code. I picked it up. On the other end, I heard a frantic voice filled with panic and emotion, once familiar and comforting: Sanjeev Mama, my mom's brother. He could barely speak.

I said, "Sanjeev Mama, it's Raam."

My dad always said he hated these types of calls. So, at this point, I knew this wasn't a happy call. "Hi, beta, mummy chai. Pappa is in the hospital."

"Is everything okay?" I asked.

There was silence, followed by muffled sounds and the phone being passed to someone else.

At this time, a light came on, and Dad and Mom came into the kitchen from different rooms, rubbing their eyes. Mom saw the terrified expression on my face.

Sanjeev Mama's wife, Payal Mami, got on the call. She was trying to be calm, but her voice was also broken.

"Dada is in critical shape."

"Is he okay?" I asked.

My dad approached me. I passed him the phone. I didn't know what to say.

"Payal, what happened?"

"Pappa is in the ICU."

I saw Mom's eyes were frantic. She overheard through the speaker.

And we all heard it—the news.

My mom collapsed on the sofa while Dad tried to wrap his arm around her. Her face was drained of any color. I was paralyzed in disbelief. My brain felt frozen, and I felt numb throughout my body.

My dad tried to get more details. Everything was fractured, and details trickled in. Mom tried to talk to Bha. They were both crying.

He had finished his chai, gone for a walk, and listened to the soundtrack of *Pyassa*, his favorite Bollywood movie soundtrack. Then he had grabbed the table and collapsed. He had always had diabetes, and I remembered Mom had injected him in the arm with insulin when we visited.

Mom was inconsolable and quiet. Dad tried to say things to comfort her, and I did too. We were all in our own world of grief. All I could think about was that swing and him telling me the stories of Hanuman. I remembered Mom trying to book a ticket to India and having difficulty because she had recently become an American citizen a month before. Her paperwork was still being processed. She needed a visa. And the only place we could get one in forty-eight hours was in Miami, which would require us to drive there and return on the same day. The crazy thing is I had never gone there, and neither had my parents.

There was silence throughout the entire trip. Everything felt drained. We stopped by a rest stop area and got doughnuts, and Mom let her coffee go cold. Dad tried to talk with her, but she was silent. Even to me, she was distant.

We went to the immigration office and waited for what felt like hours. Dad and I were sitting in the rest area on the floor, me playing on his phone. Mom finally got her visa, and we tried to go to South Beach and see the street. I remember how bright and cheap it looked the second time we drove by. We walked to the beach, and Dad tried to have Mom smile in a photo, and she tried. On our way back, we ended up lost. Later, we found this Italian restaurant and ate this fantastic gnocchi Mom loved. It was the worst day of our lives. That pasta dish somehow saved us.

My bha, Mom's mom, came to live with us for three months last year. She stayed in the guest room, and we had fun going to all the theme parks. She and my other grandma ended up hanging out, and it was a happy time. Since she left, Mom's been different.

Now it's a year later.

"Okay," I say.

Mom's already at the temple, and she will meet us after her class.

It's going to be Dad and me in the car.

Even though he's shaved, he still looks like he hasn't slept. I know he doesn't eat properly at all.

Over the last few years, he has seemed disinterested in everything. When he and Mom aren't fighting, they are silent. I almost prefer them arguing.

I overheard them speaking and talking about seeing someone to help them. I'm not sure if that ever happened. As of late, Mom has driven me everywhere, and Dad is like a ghost who comes by to visit even though he lives here.

This hasn't always been the case. We used to be inseparable.

Dad would drive me to preschool. Our thing was music, and he'd educate me and play Eminem and Prince and the Killers while I sat in my car seat and asked who the real Slim Shady was.

I remember my teacher said I had the dopest taste in music. Even during elementary school, he'd drop me off. We'd park at the golf clubhouse, and he'd hold my hand and walk me to the gate. I remember him lingering and ensuring I was on my way to class.

Mom and Dad loved to go with me to the Disney parks. We'd go almost every weekend to Magic Kingdom, EPCOT, MGM—as they still called it—and Animal Kingdom, and we'd ride one or two rides, take a photo, and watch the fireworks. We gave up those annual passes a few years ago, and I still miss those days, even though I told them I was too old.

Dad takes the Hyundai, and we leave.

He gets sentimental sometimes during drives because he grew up here in Orlando. He even went to Southwest Middle School as I do. He left and returned, which affected him because he had always said he could never go home again. He avoids socializing. Mom thinks he's embarrassed he didn't make it big in LA. He and Mom lived there for ten years and moved back after I was born because Dada and Bha were here and had family support. Mom said LA was fun, but it was lonely. They don't say much more about the move.

Dad brings water, and I take a sip.

We pass by San Jose, a Mexican restaurant. I point.

"Remember that place?" I ask.

Dad's eyes sparkle.

"Yeah, that was our go-to before we saw any movie. Best chicken enchiladas ever. They had that incredible verde sauce."

"Yup, and don't forget their famous ice cream churros."

We both grin until we see the CLOSED sign.

"Bummer," Dad says.

Twenty minutes later, Dad pulls into a side street, and we drive on a long dirt road with tons of oak trees and moss covering it. A clearing opens up.

There are two temples in Orlando. There's the local mandir, where I'm in the spelling bee camp, and the enormous complex on the east side of town.

This is the temple that Dad went to as a kid. It's fifteen acres big with a traditional temple with ornate marble carvings of Ganesh and Sarasvati and any Hindu god or goddess you can imagine. They brought in sculptors and decorators from India to do all the artisanal work by hand.

They have a giant hall for weddings and birthdays, prayer rooms, a courtyard, classrooms, and a basketball gym. They also have a restaurant that serves vegetarian food, including these fantastic dosas they offer for delivery service.

The parking lot is full. Dad and I get out.

We walk in. Shoe racks fill with sneakers, slippers, and heels. I notice half a dozen pairs of Aron's kicks.

The tulsi bush sits in front, Lakshmi's avatar. I step barefoot onto the cold marble floor. There are ornate columns and arches. Inside, men and women sit on separate sides. There are different areas of worship and murtis. A priest in orange is chanting in Sanskrit. I spot Mom in a light blue Punjabi sitting across from us.

Dad nudges me forward.

We sit. I can smell the camphor and sandalwood. The sweet scent relaxes me. Behind the priest is a pile of dishes with fruit, prasada for the gods.

One uncle, who looks my grandfather's age in a polo shirt and slacks, settles next to Dad. He whispers something to him. Dad fakes a smile.

The uncle taps me on the shoulder.

"I saw your video," he says. "Very embarrassing. I asked the pandit to say a prayer for you."

I stare at him, not believing what I had heard. Dad shakes his head.

I turn around and look at the statues. I hope they offer me sympathy.

A minute later, the pandit recites prayers for Apple Dada.

My grandpa's photo appears on a screen in front. The pandit says a blessing for him.

Mom holds back tears.

I feel a sense of emptiness as well.

After, he says blessings for others, including the sick.

The pandit points in my direction. The lights are aimed at me. Everyone turns their head.

Great. I look at Dad. He looks away, pretending not to know me.

The pandit starts to talk in Gujarati, English, and Sanskrit.

"Let's pray for one of our own, Raam Patel, and offer a blessing."

Aushman bhava!
Jeevetam sharadah shatam!
Om shanti, shanti, shanti!

All these people look at me. Dad can't even look me in the eye. Mom bites her lip and offers me sympathy.

I didn't ask for this. I can't stand it anymore, and I run outside the exit.

The temple is a wonderland of areas, and I dash anyplace I can avoid people and the limelight.

Unfortunately, I run into the worst area possible—the playground and gym. A basketball game is going on, and the kids stop when they see me. It's a 3-on-3 game, and One-Up and his brother spot me.

They point and mock. And before I can sprint from there, I turn, and right in front of me with her phone and wearing a purple Punjabi is Reena.

She is standing in front of a table for donations and spots me. Two or three other girls surround her. They all laugh in my direction. She looks at her phone and me.

"You should start a charity for him!" someone shouts.

Reena starts to laugh.

I put my head down and run off as fast as possible toward the car, tears streaming down my face. Out of breath, I want to escape.

I crouch by our tires and wait until my parents come back. Hiding by the car seems to be my go-to place for solitude.

Dad doesn't look at me when they arrive, and Mom offers me prasada.

"I can't take this anymore," I say to them. My hands are clenched. My breathing is hard, like I'm getting strangled. And I feel like I'm going to faint.

"I'm embarrassed, Raam," Dad says. "You can't act like this."

"You're embarrassed?" I yell. "You aren't infamous."

"Raam, it's going to be okay," Mom says. "This will all blow over."

"No, it's not," I scream. I want to pull my hair out.

"Get in the car," Dad says, trying to avoid the stares of the people around us.

"Please, Raam," Mom pleads. "Just get in the car."

GONE FISHING

My phone buzzes again. It's Trina. I refuse to look at it. I don't want to talk to anyone.

I've become a full-fledged recluse. I want to become one of those monks I saw in a National Geographic documentary who retreat to the mountains and live alone in the forest away from all of society.

I've barricaded myself in my room with endless games of *NBA3K*. I get tired of using my avatar to dunk on Payton, especially when I hear my parents yelling. Even through noise-cancelling headphones, their decibel level is audible.

"We are never on the same page," Dad says from the kitchen.

"Stop blaming me for your issues," Mom responds.

Even when I'm in the bathroom, their squabbling continues through the door.

"Quit, then. You're not doing me any favors," Mom says through the wall.

"Are we just co-parenting?" Dad asks.

A moment later, there are two loud door slams followed by a thump of a fallen object.

I take off the headphones and slowly open the door. It's quiet now. Too quiet.

My stomach churns. I feel dizzy, and my chest tightens like I'm batter in a waffle iron. I feel like they're arguing even more because of me. I find the door leading to the garage and the garage door itself open. Both cars are gone. I close the doors and notice a giant hole in the laundry room wall where the knob punctured the drywall. That's going to need to be patched.

I walk over to the front entrance. It's still open. The impact of the door slam knocked a painting to the ground. I pick it up.

It's a still life of a fisherman on a boat on the waves with a nearby beach. We bought this when we went to the Florida Keys when I was in fourth grade. It was a fun trip where we tagged along with Dad as he checked out a new resort where we watched the sunrise and snorkeled. The resort wasn't even done; there was construction, fresh grass, and a lot of gnats, but we had the whole villa to ourselves with the private marina and spa service that Mom loved. And it was all free.

We then went farther into the Keys over the one-lane Highway 1 that smelled of salt water and looked like it could be sunk by a hurricane. We visited the Ernest Hemingway house, one of Dad's favorite writers, where we saw the home with its arched windows and verandas, pool gardens, and six-toed cats roaming around the property that caused my allergies to go berserk.

Dad bought a painting of a man fishing on a boat from a street artist. He said it looked like a scene from a book called *The Old Man and the Sea*. Things were happy at that moment for all of us. It's not that way anymore.

Now the painting lies askew on the ground. I put it back on the wall.

After that trip, Dad got into fishing. We went to Bass Pro Shops and bought a rod, spincast reel, tackle box, bobbers, and other gear. I loved the Let's Go Fishing game when I was a kid, so I also got into it. We went a few times to the lake, but Dad got bored and agitated and stopped going after he didn't catch anything. For me, it was fun. It was relaxing. And I got to spend time with him. I heard people got so absorbed in the fishing that there was no room for other thoughts.

That sparks an idea. I go to the storage closet and find my rod. I haven't used it in what feels like years. It's rusty and tangled in string.

I'm not an expert fisherman by any means. We have fishing areas around Blake Lake and several ponds around the golf course. Occasionally, Cake and I will go out and try to catch crappie. We only end up hooking small sunfish with spiky fins that cut our hands.

I grab the reel. It's a little small but usable. I need bait: no worms or crazy rubber toys. I always used bread, and fresh white bread is always the secret. I journey into the kitchen and grab an extra loaf Mom got BOGO from Publix. I also take a water bottle to drink and moisten the bread.

The path to the lake cuts through the backyard. I bounce through the screen door onto the soggy grass. There's mud all over my shoes.

However, the hedges of the fairway are scorched. It's as dry as a desert. It hasn't been sprinkled in more than two years, and all you see are weeds, anthills, and an occasional golf ball that some neighbor must have hit, thinking it's Topgolf.

I walk down the cracked sidewalk. The dried fronds of the palm trees squeak like bad brakes as the breeze rustles through. It's sad to see all the decay and rot. I can't help feeling this is the landscape in my head.

I'm doing my best not to think about all these thoughts. I spy the shadows of the birds on the grass as they hover, wings stretched, looking for some prey. I keep extra vigilant for the cranes and the hawks with their sharp talons.

Everything feels louder and more intense as I walk.

An electric saw buzzes as workers repair a roof, and I can hear the drone of air-conditioning units. I wish there was a dial that I could turn down.

I follow the path used by golf carts, now covered in ant piles and sand swirls, to Hole 13 with its 489-yard par 5. Cake and I rode on his golf cart when we were younger. He used to steal it from his dad, and we'd sneak out late in the evening for a joyride and then hit balls into the ponds.

Weirdly, we won't be playing together. I just feel a numbness thinking about it. My ribs begin to tighten. Just like that, we aren't friends anymore. Like losing a backcourt mate, which he was.

Above me, large towering oaks stand, and the moss dangles down like creepy wizard beards. Suddenly, something wiggles in front of me, and I shriek. It's a snake. It's small, skinny, and black and wriggles into the grass.

Snakes have a peculiar relationship in our household. If you dream about a snake, it's worrisome, but if you can find one, it's good luck. Mom always burns a candle if she spots one, and in Florida, she burns a lot of candles.

I have to fight the feeling it's an omen.

Farther along Hole 14, 541 yards, par 5, a scurry of squirrels crawls up a screen porch. I hear a loud grinding sound of a dump truck followed by a loud pop and horn from the street outside. I flinch. And take a breath.

In my mind, I'm in the middle of center court, and everyone in the stands is mocking, laughing, and booing me, from Cake to Payton, to Aron, to my parents. I shut my eyes, but then I hear the loud clangor behind me. The second I look back, a woman on a bicycle whiffs past me, honking and mumbling something about getting out of the way.

I once heard from someone that you shouldn't look back because you never know what's chasing you.

I have to rest a second as I see the lady recede farther up ahead. I don't know why everything is becoming distorted and grotesque, like I am walking through the desert and seeing warped visions as I become more delirious. Mushrooms pop up like fresh mozzarella in the grass, ready to throw on a pizza. After all, it might just be the heat. I'm sweating, and the rod begins to feel heavier in my hands.

I finally see the drawbridge leading to the dock. I'm near the front of the neighborhood and can see the entrance gate. This body of water is a man-made pond and acts as a moat for the rest of the inlet. The bridge itself looks like it belongs on a pirate ship. It's decaying and dried. The nails are rusting.

In front of it is a sign: NO FISHING. CROSS AT YOUR OWN RISK. WATCH OUT FOR ALLIGATORS.

There is a neighborhood gator, and recent photos show him hanging out in this area. I look around the shore and into the water that ripples with green algae.

I see the warning, but honestly, all the damage is done. I don't know what else more I can lose—even a limb.

I take a breath and decide to cross the bridge. The planks crack under my feet. I'm in some adventure movie looking for a buried treasure. Halfway across, I hear a loud splash like something entered the water. I turn and see a turtle. His head popped above the surface and dips below.

Finally, I'm across, right near the lake.

And as I walk forward, something cathartic begins to infiltrate my body. I feel lighter, as if layers of clothing are being removed. I can smell the fresh water of the lake.

Now I'm back on land and walk across the sidewalk and shore. This area is like an overgrown oasis. One of the hidden gems of the neighborhood is the dock. It's barely used anymore. Though the wood needs another coat of paint, it has tranquility.

The seagrass is taller than Shaq and reaches over the railing as if to grab you. I feel like that guy from *Gladiator* walking through stalks of wheat. I can see the complete 180 of the lake and the houses along the shore with their boats and Jet Skis.

These are all lakefront properties across the bay. There's no one under the canopy of the dock. I finally feel a little easier. I take some bread out and toss the crumbs into the water. I redo the bait and cast the line near some lily pads. Boats and Jet Skis speed by in the distance. I hear the waves sloshing back and forth.

As I wait, I spot graffiti etched into the bench.

UR MOM
DON'T WORRY, BE HAPPY.
JOJO'S BIZARRE IS THE BEST NAME EVER.

The second message seems like it's directly for me. Part of me wished I had a broad-brimmed straw hat and a huge cane pole. But I instead cast my rod with all my might. I hope I catch something. I watch the bob on the surface, and a few seconds later, I feel a pull.

I love the movement of basketball, the various speeds and pressures, and the constant motion. It's like life where you're always going like a fast break, never stopping. I have trouble taking things slowly.

Fishing is different. It requires slowing down and being patient. Honestly, I wish I could play like I fish. I'm in a tranquil state. No noise, simply waiting for a bite. And then the peaceful feeling of water and the pull and tug.

Fishing is my fortress of solitude. Someone called it flow, this mindset where nothing matters, everything falls away, and you are just focused. No room for thought, and everything else fades by. I feel that now. I remember Kobe, MJ, and all these other athletes talking about being in the zone. It's the same.

A big open-mouth bass emerges from the water. I'm reeling it in when an eagle comes soaring down and rips it from my rod. I watch it flap its wings. The fish is trapped between its beak. The eagle flies away.

But I'm not upset or mad. Honestly, it's okay. I don't feel a rush, excited, or disappointed. Just chill.

I try a few more times. No bites. Finally, I get a nibble and start reeling in the fish, not with a frantic rush but slowly.

I pull it up finally, and then the fish comes up. The crappie is small, not too big. It flaps its tail.

I grab the hook from its mouth and hold it in my grip. The

gills and scales shimmer. I stare at it, then let it go. I've never had a more serene feeling. I want to hold on to it for as long as I can.

For so long, I've been swimming against the current. Now I think I need to swim with it.

A minute later, the air starts to get heavy. My moment is fading, but I want to return to it as soon as possible.

As I'm walking back home, I notice my basketball in the seaweed sloshing back and forth in the water trapped in the mangroves. It's too far for me to reach it.

Suddenly, I hear rustling from a bush and see a family of ducks waddle into the water: two adults and four baby ducklings. I'm astonished for a second. They look like newborns. I'm not even sure they can fly yet. They look happy and carefree.

The walk back home is long and hotter. I cut through a yard, and a landscaping guy yells at me.

In front of all the houses are green garbage cans waiting to be emptied. I finally get near the driveway and notice Mom and Dad are both home now. I head inside.

They both sit on opposite sides of the dining table. It feels like they were waiting for me to get back home. Something is clearly on their minds.

"Hey, Raam," Dad says. "We need to talk."

I'm still feeling sticky and sweaty. The stress I had now comes back like the tide. I don't need more of it.

"Yes, raja," Mom says as well.

I have a deep fear about what's coming next.

"Your mom and I wanted to let you know that we need to take some time for ourselves this month."

I'm beginning to feel nauseous.

"Oh, does that mean you're separating?" I ask.

"No, sweetie," Mom says. "We aren't, but we need to figure some things out between your dad and me."

"We are trying to make things work," Dad says. "But we need time."

"So, what does that mean?"

"Raam, I'm getting tired of you skulking around like Howard Hughes all day," Dad says.

"Who?" I ask.

"Never mind," he says. "You need a change too."

"Well, we talked to your Mahendra Uncle and Neela Kaki,"

Mom says. "And we are sending you to visit them in California for the month."

"Wait, I get to stay with Trina?" I ask.

"Yes."

I'm not upset, honestly. I need to escape from Orlando. I've already been embarrassed, lost my best friend, and refused to leave the house. I'm not sure what to feel. I crack my knuckles. They're kicking me out of the house, but simultaneously I get excited that I can finally make it out to the West Coast. Since the beginning of Hoop Con, it's the first time I've felt excited.

"Got it."

"We think it would be good for you and us."

"I'm okay with this."

"We're glad to hear."

"You know you haven't been back there since you left to move here," Mom says with a smile.

"It will be nice."

It's odd. They thought I'd be upset, but I'm not. I'm relieved.

I text Trina when I get back to my room.

While I'm running all these thoughts in my head, I get a text from her.

ME: **I'm coming to LA!**

TRINA: **That's why I kept messaging you.**

ME: **Sorry.**

TRINA: **You're gonna be like the Fresh Prince coming home.**

ME: **I like that.**

TRINA: **Tru! Tru! Cali, Cali. We keep it rocking.**

I fall asleep dreaming of California as the neighborhood bursts with the sound of Disney fireworks in the distance.

ESCAPE TO LA

Sunbursts flicker through the trees.

We're on our way to the airport.

I have an early 8 a.m. flight to Los Angeles, and Mom and Dad are driving me in the minivan. My suitcase is in the back, clothes packed for a month.

Trina says she and Neela Kaki will pick me up outside the airport arrival area.

Mom's worried I'll get lost in LA and that the city will consume me.

"You're like your dad. You would get lost in your own driveway, let alone a big city," she tells me as we leave our neighborhood.

Dad rolls his eyes as we jump on the highway.

I haven't flown anywhere since I went to India years ago. And I don't remember my trip from Los Angeles to Orlando when I was two.

I recall a photo Mom took of me in a stroller in front of a WELCOME TO ORLANDO sign when we landed. It always pops up in her memories reminder on her phone.

I see billboards of Aron on the road promoting season tickets. There's a brand-new one being put up for Dunkin. I think I inspired it.

As we take the exit to the airport, planes zoom overhead, engines buzzing like an electric razor.

"Do you guys miss LA?" I ask both of them.

Mom looks into the rearview mirror, chews her lips, and looks back to Dad. He pauses and taps the steering wheel. I didn't know it was such a complicated question.

"You mean the earthquakes, droughts, wildfires, and high taxes," Dad says, laughing.

Even Mom smirks.

"The answer is yes," he says, staring ahead at the road.

"I miss it too," Mom concurs. "I miss a lot about it. The freedom, the creativity, the weather."

"The food too," Dad says.

"Tacos!" they both say simultaneously.

They crack a smile, something I haven't seen in a while.

"So why did you leave?" I ask.

We drive toward the gate for my airline. It's empty.

"It's complicated," Mom says.

Dad pulls the car to the passenger loading area. A police officer guides traffic.

"Well, kiddo, we had our adventure in California, and now so will you," Dad says, avoiding my question.

He pops the trunk.

We all get out and retrieve my bag.

Mom hugs me, and Dad rubs my head as he did when I was little.

Mom tries to hide tears. Her mascara runs down her face. She hands me the small Krishna murti I had from my locker. They both look exhausted. My chest feels an ache, and I know why. I don't want to say it.

They both wave to me from the car as I enter the double doors of the airport. They're probably waiting till I go in before they leave. I give another glance, and they're gone.

As soon as I get in line to check in my baggage and print my ticket, a kid wearing multicolored socks similar to Payton's stands in front of me. For a second, I'm filled with fear and dread. This can't be my fate. If he turns around and sees me, it's over. Luckily, it's some older guy with bad fashion sense.

I make my way past security, shoes off. I have Sky Hardaways on. They are the only shoes I own. I pass by the Disney Store, hotel, and food courts and take the tram to my gate. Over the intercom, the mayor says *thank you for visiting* as I grip the safety bar and glide over a pond to the Delta terminal.

I stop at a newsstand to buy gum and water. In front of me, near the register, are basketball magazines with Aron on the cover. I flip through and see a photo with Aron and Payton from the camp. I put it down and leave, almost forgetting to pay.

At the gate, I sit and listen to the playlist Trina sent me. It's all LA-based music, from '90s rockers like the Red Hot Chili Peppers and Tom Petty to rappers like Tupac and Nipsey Hussle. Trina says I have to understand the entire vibe of LA, and music is the best way. She's an old soul, as she likes to say.

I have a window seat, so I stare outside as the clouds morph and change into various figures and animals. The guy in a suit sitting in the aisle seat watches TV.

It's an on-demand screen, and he turns on a top ten sports show. I fear my clip might be on there.

I turn to the window and pretend to sleep, avoiding the flight attendant bringing pretzels and drinks. I drift off. The humming of the plane eases me into slumber.

A loud jolt knocks me awake as the flight attendant tells us to buckle our belts because we are experiencing turbulence. I grip my armrests. Luckily, the plane settles down.

An unfamiliar landscape with mountain ranges and deserts greets me outside my window. The only mountains I ever see in Florida are Space and Splash-related.

I spot the NFL football stadium, the Hollywood sign, and the valley with highways everywhere.

The landing gear unwinds, and we touch down with a thump.

"Ladies and gentlemen, welcome to Los Angeles International Airport," the flight attendant announces. "The local time is twelve thirty p.m."

It feels mystical as I disembark and grab my luggage from the winding baggage carousel. Like it's all-new but familiar. I may recall some infant memory. I walk for what seems like miles and observe the constant construction.

I finally get outside and pass the taxi stand and bus area. Kaki and Trina would grab me from there.

As I wait and soak in the dry air and smog fumes, a scrum of photographers follows a girl with sunglasses around, snapping away. I notice she's this celebrity reality star I've seen on TV. Man, I haven't been here thirty minutes, and I already see paparazzi. I hope they don't recognize me.

A double honk diverts my attention, and a large SUV rolls up—a hand waves at me from outside the passenger window.

"Raam!"

It's Trina. She and Neela Kaki park and get out. I throw my bag into the trunk. Both of them give me a big hug.

Trina wears her Kobe jersey. Her wild curly hair is pulled back in a ponytail. She jumps up and down. Her energy is endless. Kaki doesn't smile at first. I can see her trying. There's no crease on her forehead.

Kaki sees me staring at her a little too intently.

"It's just numb. I had some filling," she says.

"Mom saw a wrinkle and freaked," Trina says, laughing.

"I'm an open book," Kaki says. "And we're in LA. If I didn't get Botox, I'd be the weird one."

I'm totally lost in this conversation.

The pickup area is madness, and I hear the honking and screeching of traffic. We get in the car and peel out.

"Welcome home, bro," Trina says, throwing her sunglasses on. "You are in the land of milk and honey."

"Hungry?" is the first thing Kaki asks.

"Yes, I didn't eat on the flight," I say.

"Why, beta?" Kaki asks.

"I fell asleep and didn't want anyone to recognize me."

"In LA, no one notices," Trina says. "Mom, let's ingratiate this boy to West Coast cuisine," she continues, pointing to the In-N-Out on the corner. A line stretches outside the door, and a cavalcade of cars waits at the drive-thru lane.

"Not today. I made food at home," Kaki says.

Trina scrunches her face and rolls her eyes.

"Fine, next time," she says.

"Plus, I'm trying to keep slim and trim for this wedding," Kaki says.

"What wedding?" I ask.

I know Trina isn't getting married, so it wasn't my family.

"Oh, Sunil's wedding," Trina says. "He's Mom's friend, Bina Auntie's son, but Mom is playing wedding planner, running around like a chicken with its head cut off."

Trina sounds annoyed. I notice she's constantly moving in her seat and fidgeting with her ponytail.

"It's family," Neela Kaki says. "We have a responsibility."

"You were helping with dress shopping and making puris for three hundred people."

Auntie smiles.

"I enjoy it."

"So start a business," Trina says. "And monetize it."

I look at both of them, baffled.

"Don't worry," they both say. "You're coming."

I want to nap. We aren't moving—traffic along the 405. It's the biggest highway I've ever seen. Six lanes and all of it filled with cars. The route dips down a hill into the valley.

Trina lives in "The Valley" in a city called Sherman Oaks, a suburb of Los Angeles. My parents lived in Burbank when I was born.

We get off the exit and turn on Ventura Boulevard.

It reminds me of International Drive with all the shops. These are fresher, not tacky tourist traps. I spot record shops, cafés, car washes, and more.

We pass a Cadillac dealership and hot dog stand.

I check my phone. Three missed calls from Mom.

I text her back.

ME: **Reached.**

Mom writes back.

MOM: **Have fun. West Coast. Best Coast.** 🩶

Neela Kaki pulls into a gated underground parking garage under a large pineapple-colored condo building. We pull up next to a Lamborghini. Trina notices me staring.

"Oh, that belongs to MC Legend," she says casually. "He lives on the same floor with his mom."

I notice there are several nice rides. And no minivans.

I grab my bag.

Outside the entry door is an empty swimming pool. We take

the elevator up to the third floor. There are five units, and we walk to the last door.

Kaki opens it up. As soon as she does, I glimpse a swift motion of a creature leaping at me, nearly causing me to fall. The slobbery tongue of a dog licks my face as I try to regain my balance.

"Bean, get off him," Trina says, laughing as she moves the dog off me.

Bean is excited and starts barking. He has a coat of golden curly hair the color of fried chicken.

Mom and Dad would never get a pet. I'm allergic to cats but, thank god, not dogs. Bean is adorable.

"He's very friendly and very naughty," Trina says. "I do love him so much."

"What kind of dog is he?" I ask.

"Goldendoodle. Part golden retriever and poodle. He's only a year old."

"Yes, and he eats all my pillows," Kaki says.

"He's a total goober," Trina says, rubbing his belly. "Aren't you?"

Trina throws a chew toy into the living room.

"He doesn't want to retrieve it. More like catch it once, then you chase him! He loves 'playing chase'—so he takes his toy and runs for you to run after him."

I look around and notice the condo's interior is a penthouse with tall ceilings and a spiral staircase. Initially, everything is neatly organized and stylish, like one of those magazines showing celebrity homes. I notice basketball equipment everywhere and a pile of Amazon boxes containing pizza cutters when I look closer.

"What do you think?" Auntie says.

She holds one up. It says SWATI WEDS SUNIL and the wedding date.

"It's cool. What's it for?"

"Wedding gift for guests. Who doesn't love or need a pizza cutter?"

Trina rolls her eyes.

"Where's Uncle?" I ask.

"Dad's coming back from picking up groceries. He saw a recipe for lamb kebabs on *Super Chef* that he wants to make."

Trina tells me to put my bag down.

"Let me give you a tour of mi casa," she says.

She's taller than me and full of untamed energy like Tigger. I mean, she's always moving even when she's still, like she's always on the cusp of telling you about her day like a toddler. It's infectious. She's also as big of a basketball fan as I am and my go-to expert for game knowledge. Bean follows us.

I follow her up the winding staircase to the loft area. Upstairs is an office with shelves of books all organized by color. Kaki is a huge reader.

Trina opens a door on the same floor and leads me outside.

"Check this out," she says, her face beaming.

I follow her onto the rooftop deck that overlooks the mountain and the valley.

"Those are the San Gabriel Mountains. At night, you can see the lights of those million-dollar actor houses glitter. It's very bougie."

I've never seen a view like this before.

"You're gonna have a blast," she says. "And trust me, you need it. I'm glad you're here."

She elbows me on the shoulder, grinning.

"I have big plans for us."

"Like what?" I ask. Nervous.

"You'll see," she says, teasing me about the upcoming adventures.

I follow her downstairs into her room as she hops down the steps like a kangaroo.

If my room was an Aron exhibit, Trina's room is a museum to Kobe. Though Kobe is gone, she remains a dedicated fan. Her room is filled with Kobe posters, a #24 Bryant rug, sneakers, and a large photo of her meeting Kobe, his daughter Gigi, and her teammates. Kobe smiles and shakes her hand. I stare at it.

Bean comes by my side. I scratch his ears.

"Gigi was as cool if not cooler than her dad," Trina says. "And that's hard to beat. She mentored me when I was younger."

Trina stands taller when she says this. I can tell she takes pride.

"I wish this could have been a photo with Aron and me," I say glumly.

"I'm gonna give you one more chance to sulk, and then we're changing your attitude," she says as she adjusts her hair again into another updo.

"Okay," I say.

The front door opens, and Mahendra Uncle walks in. He's a giant teddy bear of a human being, and it's weird to see him as a younger version of my grandfather with a happy belly. Mahendra Uncle is the oldest family member my mom has in the United States. He was the one who introduced my mom and dad when they first met in person. My grandfather in Orlando, my dad's dad, and my uncle are from the same town in India. They tried introducing my dad and mom years ago after my dad graduated from college.

Mahendra Uncle works for LEGO®. For years, he has been an engineer there. I notice all over the house there are LEGO® sets. An oversize Taj Mahal, a Stormtrooper helmet, and a British guard award celebrating his tenth anniversary at the company.

Uncle has a joyful laugh and busts my chops.

"You have become quite the celebrity. You'll fit right in to LA."

Uncle and Kaki were like surrogate parents to my parents in LA. That's what both Mom and Dad agree on.

"Raam, I picked up some papaya for the lamb kebab marinade. I will make it one of these days. I just got a tandoori oven," Uncle says.

"But today," Kaki says, "we feast Gujarati style."

While eating again at the dining table, Kaki made an entire Guju meal. I don't like Guju cuisine, which bothers Mom, but with Kaki, you eat everything, every morsel and crumb on your plate. I devour the kadhi, puri, and shrikhand. Uncle pours himself and Kaki red wine.

"We got this pinot from Santa Barbara last weekend when we went wine tasting."

I have no idea what he's talking about.

A knock on the door interrupts us.

Trina gets up.

Uncle and Kaki continue as if nothing happened.

Trina springs up from her seat like a jack-in-the-box and opens the door. A brunette-haired girl with french braids walks in.

She's super cute. I feel a tingle, and the hair on my arms stands up.

I nearly drop my plate, Trina laughs, and the girl giggles.

"Um, Allie, meet my nephew slash cousin, Raam," Trina says, grabbing my head and giving me a noogie.

"Heard a lot about you," she says, smiling. "You're the one who plays ball, right?"

"Yeah, a little," I say, pulling myself from Trina's grasp.

I don't want to look at Allie too directly because she's making me nervous.

Not even Reena had that effect immediately.

"Raam, meet my BFF, Allie."

I knew of Allie. I'd seen her on Instagram posts.

"Did you hear about the audition?" Trina asks.

"Yup, I have a callback tomorrow. Fingers crossed," Allie says.

I raise my eyebrow.

Trina notices.

"Allie's auditioning for a Disney Channel show as the lead," she says.

"Oh, awesome," I say. "Good luck."

"Thanks!" she says. "Are we still going to the sneaker drop?"

"Yup. Going to show this kid that LA is the vibe."

I look at her, clueless about what she's talking about.

Allie gets a text on her phone.

"Crap, I have to go. Mom needs me to get some food."

"Just order Uber Eats."

"She doesn't believe in that. Nice to meet you, Raam," she says, waving.

I don't want her to go.

"Bye, Allie."

She leaves.

"Oh man," Trina says, laughing.

I look at her. Uncle and Kaki also stare at me.

"What?" I say, clueless.

Kaki and Uncle start laughing too.

"That quick?" Trina says. "That look on your face says it all."

"You still have food on your plate, Raam. And on your face."

They continue to crack up.

"Raam, listen, don't get too smitten," Trina says.

My face goes red as I stare at my plate.

Later on, Uncle brings out a new LEGO® project. It's a replica of the Eiffel Tower.

LEGO® Night is something they've done as a family bonding activity since Trina was tiny. Something I wish my own family could do.

I get exhausted when I get upstairs and crash on the sofa bed. I check to see my social feeds and find a remixed video someone did with sound effects and auto-tune, and an episode of an online animated show that shows me as a cartoon. That's a first. Cake's channel has blown up even more. Even coming to LA, I can't escape what's chasing me.

MAMBACITA MENTALITY

A bright, blinding light waves over me. Either I'm dreaming, or a UFO is abducting me. An extraterrestrial that looks like a Wookiee stares at me and licks my face.

It disappears until I notice it's a cell phone. Trina's and Bean's faces appear in the dark, nudging me to wake up.

"Everything okay?" I ask. "What's going on?"

I'm groggy, and it's pitch-dark outside.

"Wakey wakey, eggs and bakey," Trina says, her eyes beaming.

"For what?"

"Training?" she says. "Every day, like Kobe. I should have left an hour ago. I wanted to give you a little break."

I look at the clock. It's 4 a.m.

"You get up at three?"

"Have to outwork the competition and keep peak readiness. I can always take a fifteen-minute nap later on."

"Okay, you're insane."

I put the blanket over my head to avoid the eye exam.

"Raam, I know it's been tough," she says, "but we have to get you mentally and physically ready to bounce back and ball."

The throbbing reality starts oozing back into my head. Since the Payton debacle, I haven't touched a basketball. I'm done.

"My basketball career is over," I say to her. "I hung up my sneaks."

"That is nonsense and weak sauce," she insists.

"I came here to relax, rest, and escape everything."

Aside from the glow, the early morning is dark blue, and I'm still wondering if I was in a half dream.

"You can't run away from your problems."

"I wish I could," I say.

"Can't sulk, little bro. Adversity is growth," she says, tossing a ball in my direction that almost breaks my nose. I'm not a morning person, at least, not a four-in-the-morning person.

"I'm not going to embarrass myself again," I say, tossing the ball back to her.

"Fine," she says, hopefully giving up. "I'll give you two minutes to get off your butt and join me. If not, you can continue sleeping in like the other noobs."

She leaves the basketball next to me.

"I'll be outside the front door."

I can hear her and Bean descend the steps, the wood of the stairs squeaking despite them trying to keep quiet.

I lean back on the pillow and stare at the ceiling fan as it whirs above me. All I can see are feet jumping over me and all I hear is mocking and laughter. Even when I shut my eyes, I can feel the shame in my stomach and the visions coming at me no matter how I try to wipe them away.

I lean up, take a deep breath, and grab the ball.

I quietly open the front door and wear my sneakers. Trina leans on the rail, smiling like she's waiting for me.

"How did you know?"

"There was no doubt. Same bloodline," she says, crossing her arms proudly.

I pass her the basketball.

"Let's go, bruv," she says.

We emerge from the building into a neighborhood still asleep under the full moon fever. I can see the faint crack of dawn. It's tranquil; the only noise is Trina dribbling the ball.

"Why four a.m.? Do you not sleep?" I ask, still rubbing my eyes.

"I get four more hours of activity," Trina says as she pretends to shoot the ball in the air. "Kobe kept this up since high school, and look how far he went."

"Kobe was different."

"Yeah. So am I, and so are you."

I envy her. She believes what she's saying.

"Where are we heading?" I ask.

"The gym's about half a mile away," she says. "I have the code for the lock. Plus, the groundskeeper knows me."

We walk by restaurants, bars, and galleries, chairs stacked on tables, and the pavement soaked from cleaning. One coffee shop is open, and the lights are on, and we see a barista inside who waves to us.

"Does he know you?" I ask Trina.

"Yeah, he doesn't see many people this early," she says.

I don't see a soul around.

We walk past a church and a statue of Saint Teresa and see a chain-link fence and a lock. Trina takes her headband out and shakes her curls. They're exceptionally wild today.

"Mane madness," she says. "I don't know who in our genetic pool had these coils, but remind me to thank them."

She giggles, then turns the dial to the right combination, and it clicks open.

"One time, a cop thought I was breaking in," she says. "But he recognized me because his daughter plays in the same league."

We walk around the church's gym. Trina types in a number on the electronic lock, and it opens.

"Twenty-four, eight, thirty-three," she says, grinning—Kobe's uniform numbers.

We enter the lobby of a darkened gym. Trina flicks on the lights, and the entire place lights up like a Christmas tree cere-mony. The windows are arched and silhouetted by golden sparks bouncing off the hardwood. We truly are in a holy cathedral.

I hear the solitary screech of my sneaker. I'm still wearing the Arons.

"So we're gonna shoot?" I ask, still taking measured steps. I imagine the gym is packed with campers laughing at me. I need to calm these thoughts.

"No, we're gonna run," she says. "We're going to do cardio. I'm going to have you sprint with me."

"Why?"

"Because I signed us up to play in Ballerfest."

"You did what?" I ask, dumbfounded.

"Thought you should get your game back on, and what better venue."

Ballerfest is one of the biggest 3-on-3 streetball tournaments globally that takes place in LA every year. There were thousands of participants. Even Aron played in it when he was younger.

I can't believe she did this.

"No way I'm playing," I say.

No freaking way.

"You are," she says, tossing me the ball. "You don't know it yet. First, let's stretch."

I touch my toes and stretch my hamstrings and calves.

"All right, let's do this!" Trina says, letting out a primal scream.

She bolts. I try to catch up with her. She moves like a rabbit through the grass, swift and smooth.

Twenty seconds later, I'm out of breath, and she stops and looks at me, disappointed.

"Can't get lazy. We're not even halfway through, and you're gasping for air."

"This. Is. Insane," I utter.

"Peak performance," she says, grinning as she puts her hands on her knees. She keeps tapping her feet.

I take another breath and follow her. Her stamina is bananas.

"Gotta push your limits," she says. "Gotta outwork the competition."

"You're repeating everything in Kobe's book," I say.

She smiles and barely breaks a sweat.

"Of course, I'm a disciple, but my training comes from a Mambacita twist."

At least, she admits to it. I remember Aron talking about how much Kobe inspired him and how he once played against him. I can use some of that.

Trina grabs the ball and passes it to me. My hands sting. Not sure what she put on it.

"Let's start near the basket and work back," she says, pointing. "Basic fundies."

We start in the paint and start hitting shots. Easy and harder. Her shot is smooth, and I can see hours of practice in the fluidity of her follow-through.

We do this for about five minutes, and I'm getting bored.

It's all getting repetitive.

"How many do we have to do?" I ask.

"I usually do five hundred," she says nonchalantly as she drains another shot. No net.

"Wait, what?" I ask, turning to her. Girl is absurd.

"I want to outwork my competition," she says. "You're only at one hundred."

She winks. And then shoots.

Begrudgingly, I finish the drill. I'm exhausted. I collapse on the floor and have a tremendous urge to sleep right there.

I check the clock. It's already 8 a.m. I grab a sip of water from the fountain.

Trina and I are setting up for cone drills when we hear the echo of a basketball hitting the floor.

"I thought it was only us," I say, slightly spooked.

"Me too," Trina says, her brow wrinkling.

A tall guy approaches from the tunnel. He wears a Magic Johnson jersey and has mini braids. He looks like he's a senior in high school.

Trina narrows her lips and glares.

"Great, this guy," she says, looking at me.

Before I can ask, he spots us.

"How did you sneak in here?" he asks, smirking. "That's breaking and entering. I should call the cops and have you arrested."

"I have permission."

"Well, time for you and the other scrub to leave," he says as he jumps up and grabs the rim, pulling himself up.

This guy reminds me of the Moores, except bigger.

He spots me while still on the rim and looks at me curiously.

"Yo, are you that kid Payton Newman clowned?"

He starts laughing like a hyena.

"Man, I would be too scared to show my face."

"Your point, Eric? He's my cousin."

Great. I look at Trina, who remains nonchalant and stone-faced. With her hands on her hips, I don't think she will take crap from anyone, including him.

I'm done listening to it. I can feel this pressure in my skull and my skin heating up.

"We aren't leaving. Afraid we'll beat you?"

"You got some guts, little man," he says.

"Let's get this over with," I say, walking over to this guy who is taller than me. I throw the ball at him.

"Raam," Trina says, laughing. "Raam, dude, we are just playing."

I look at her, and she's on the ground cracking up, like knee-slapping guffawing. I'm utterly confused and look at them both. She finally gets up, readjusting her hair into a giant bun that sits on her head like a hat.

"Raam, relax," Eric says. "My name is Eric. I'm Trina's friend. I was messing with you."

His smarmy look has now transformed into a sympathetic smile.

He reaches out his hand. I hesitate to shake it.

"My bad, bro," he says. "No harm, no foul."

"We wanted to get you motivated. Not riled up," Trina says. "This is when we talk about regulating your intensity."

"Well, it riled me up," I say.

Trina puts her arm around me.

"Little bro," she says. "You must learn how to attack this weakness and use it as fuel. The wound is still fresh. I can see now. Let's chill for a bit and get something to eat."

It takes me a few more minutes to regain balance and realize that Trina and Eric were busting my chops. I practice for another hour with them. Trina and Eric can play, and their camaraderie is genuine on the court. They feed off each other like Cake and I did when we were a team and still friends.

"So, Raam, Eric will be our other teammate," Trina says.

She's still strong-arming me to play. I know she's persistent, but she's verging on annoying.

"No way," I say. "Practice is one thing. A tournament is another."

"Don't make a decision yet," Eric says to me. "Keep an open mind, practice with us, and we'll see."

Nah, I'm good. I'm utterly exhausted, we're finally done.

"I can't believe it's already Tuesday," Eric says, checking his phone.

Trina's eyes bug out.

"Tuesday?" she says, surprised. "You know what today is, right?"

Eric laughs and looks at me.

"Time to bust some wax," he says.

I have no idea what he means.

"The shop must be open," Trina says as she grabs the ball and nudges me as I tie my shoe. "Let's go, dude. Don't have a minute to waste."

WAX ON, WAX OFF

Trina is full of surprises, and I have no idea where we're going.

I haven't been in Los Angeles for more than twenty-four hours.

This place is like a different planet, an extraordinary, surreal, fascinating new world with a vast diversity of humanity and geography. The vibe is different. The air is different. The palm trees are different.

Trina bounds ahead while Eric and I talk. I notice right away that the guy doesn't seem to walk. He seems to glide in his sneakers as if skating on ice. And he wears a pair of Aron Limiteds. They're ultra-rare.

"I picked them up at a sneaker drop last year," he tells me.

He's a sneakerpedia and tells me all about the history of Aron's sneakers. Some of which I didn't even know.

"They're dropping a new pair of XJs on Friday in Westwood," he says. "You should come with Trina."

"Don't worry, we'll check it out," Trina says as we cross the light. She's still dribbling like it's breathing, even with cars around.

Eric tells me he lives in the building right across from Trina.

"We've known each other since elementary school," he says.

Though he looks much older, he's just two years older than I am. He and Trina are the same age.

Both of them played for their school teams. They seem to be like the Moores but cooler and more likable.

Trina, Eric, and I walk down Ventura Avenue. The morning is kicking. The sky is bright blue.

I see Casa Vega, the famous Mexican restaurant in that Leonardo DiCaprio movie, and its neon blue-and-pink sign.

"Bro," Eric says, "Casa Vega is great, but there's a legendary taco truck called Aunt Chiladas. This abuela makes the best shrimp tacos you have ever had. You never know where they will be; she does only one weekly appearance. I heard she's gonna be in this area today."

LA is a foodie's paradise, I heard. I remember Mom and Dad binging on food shows where they talked about all the legendary Angelino joints.

The street is alive with action. There's a car wash already lined up with rides ready to get waxed and detailed. We pass gyms, sushi joints, and organic supermarkets and finally see a small shopping strip next to a laundromat and a florist shop. There's a red awning with a sign that says:

COLLECTOR'S KINGDOM: CARDS, COMICS, AND MEMORABILIA

Posters of Kobe's rookie card and Aron and others like Mickey Mantle appear on the front windows.

Trina puts her hand on the door and puts her finger to her lip to shush us before we go in. There must be something top secret going on.

As we enter, I hear the famous Chicago Bulls championship theme music go off like a ringtone. The first thing I notice is the floor. The wood of a basketball court stretches all the way down the store.

Inside, price guides are organized on the wall next to hobby supplies. On the left side are pallets of wax boxes piled on top of each other. Discount packs for a buck are stacked in bins along with albums with glossy photos and plenty of memorabilia, from helmets to jerseys. The glass display cases with single cards in slabs are on the other side.

I spot an area with Funko Pop figures and Pokémon cards. It smells like an old bookstore mixed with cotton candy and bubble gum.

A large tabletop looks like you could sit and eat on it, but it is covered in cards. This is like a paradise for any collecting nerd.

I spot Kobe jerseys that are signed, and more importantly to me, a signed pair of Aron's kicks and his rookie jersey that's mounted and framed on the wall. It looks like the sickest sports bar of all time, one where you could sit down and watch a game on the giant TV that blares highlights from ESPN.

At the other end of the store, a man with a beard and long hair who looks like he could be a roadie for a rock band sits in front of a giant display of the store's logo with camera equipment and lights set up like a small studio. Boxes of cards are stacked on the table.

I can see he's opening packs and putting them into sleeves and plastic holders.

Trina whispers to me.

"Matt's finishing up a card break," she says. "He opens packs for customers who order online and broadcasts it on the internet. Like unboxing a treasure chest."

I understood. It's like that kid who opens up toys and gets millions of views on YouTube.

A minute later, Matt takes off his headset and waves at us.

Eric analyzes all the sneakers displayed on the wall.

Matt's eyes open wide in recognition.

"Trina, been a while," the man says as he walks up and shakes Trina's hand. "Was busting a Prizm Basketball box. Busy morning."

He grabs a piece of bubble gum from a jar, unwraps it, and pops it into his mouth.

"Eric," Matt calls out, "did you see the new Jordans I got? Look up to the right."

"Sweet."

"This is my cousin Raam," Trina says. "He's from Orlando. Big Aron fan."

"Good to hear. Aron's cards have exploded in price. Check out that area over there."

He points to a glass display case.

I spot a shelf full of expensive Aron cards, some with patches of his uniform, some autographed. And I see the same card I just sold. It's a different number, but the same card. The price is one thousand dollars. That's double what I sold it for.

"See anything you like?" Matt asks.

"I had this card," I say, pointing sorrowfully.

He walks over.

"Oh, sweet card. His cards have doubled in value in the past month."

"I sold it for half that price."

He winces.

"Hey, it happens. You can never time the market. But one rule to remember. A bird in the hand is better than two in the bush."

I stare at the card again. He's right. There is no point in trying to repurchase the card. I miss it, though. At least I made five hundred dollars. I still need to figure out what to do with the money I made. I feel guilty that Mom paid for the entire Hoop Con pass that I wasted.

Matt walks over to Trina.

"So, I assume you are here to bust the pack. I got this box off auction recently. You get first dibs."

Matt goes to the back of the store and brings the box like a five-star meal on a platter.

It's a plastic-covered blue, yellow, and red wax box of Fleer 1988 basketball cards.

Trina's eyes light up, and she has this Grinch grin making a U shape on her face.

"Fresh as a Kirk Gibson World Series game-winning home run," he says.

I look at Trina. I have no idea what he's referencing.

Trina is much more of a collector than I am.

I had never seen a box this old before.

Matt takes a razor and slices the plastic off. He pops open the box.

"Premium stash. That's two hundred and fifty dollars a pack. Ten thousand a box."

"A box!" I gasp.

"That's nothing," he says, smiling, pointing to a box that looks like a heavily protected suitcase. "That Diamond box is twenty-five thousand dollars."

"Is there a diamond in there?" I ask.

Matt chuckles.

"I traded my Luka rookie for a pack," Trina says, justifying her purchase.

"High roller," Eric jokes.

"You can get a rookie John Stockton, Scottie Pippen, Reggie Miller, Dennis Rodman, and third-year Jordan," Matt explains.

Trina rubs her hands in excitement.

All of us watch, leaning in on the glass case.

"Wait for a second," Matt says abruptly. "Need to go live on this."

He brings back his phone.

"We're going handheld," he says.

Trina smiles and rummages through the box and grabs a pack.

She gently unfolds the waxy red-white-and-blue paper with

its twelve cards, one sticker, and a stick of gum inside—the paper crinkles. I can see the adhesive glue strands stretch and break and the dusty gum powder. She takes the stack in her hands like it's a sunken treasure.

She looks at me, eyes full of mischief.

"Let's make a quick wager. If I get a Jordan, you have to try the gum."

I am again under the spotlight.

"What?" I say. "That's disgusting and toxic. It's like thirty-plus years old."

She doesn't want me to survive my trip.

She flips through a few cards. Patrick Ewing sticker. Cliff Levingston, Roy Hinson. All commons.

The borders are dark in the middle and get lighter. The inner frame is colored with rounded corners. It has the player's name in an art deco font alongside the bubbly Fleer logo.

The last card is Jordan. I look at her, shocked. Her mouth is agape.

But there's a piece of gum stuck to it. Trina tries to flick the gum off, but it's bonded to the card. Half of it falls off.

She gives me half the gum.

I'm curious about what we're doing about the gum stuck on the rookie.

If in mint condition, this card is worth thousands. The stuck gum could damage the value.

"Pay up," she says. "It's only half. You got off easy."

I hesitate, but I put the loose stick on my tongue and wait for it to vanish. But it's stale as cardboard and breaks apart into particles that hijack my gums and teeth.

I nearly gag and throw up. Trina, Matt, and Eric crack up.

I go outside and spit out as much of the chalky gunk as I can, trying to rid myself of this poison. Trina comes out and tosses me a water bottle. She shakes her head at me, smiling.

I drink water and spit out the aftertaste.

"I should have just had you commit to playing in Ballerfest, instead," she says, laughing.

"Trying to poison me?" I ask, still plucking chunks of the crap from my teeth.

"No, but that was funny."

Eric bursts through the door.

"Yo, Aunt Chiladas is down the street. I saw the tweet. She's here for another few minutes. We have to get there."

Trina grabs her cards. We say bye to Matt, and we make a run for it.

Unfortunately, we miss the truck by a few minutes.

By the time we get to the location on Woodman Boulevard, we see people finishing their last bite of the tacos and wiping their faces with napkins, full and happy.

Eric is bummed. He kicks the curb, smudging his sneaks.

Trina taps him on the shoulder. She gives him a consoling look.

"We'll find her this summer. I promise."

She wipes her curls off her face and readjusts her ponytail.

"Where do you guys want to go?" I ask.

I'm still hungry.

They both look at me.

"We got you."

I still don't know what a bao is. Trina says it's an Asian bun stuffed with all sorts of ingredients.

We are at a small sit-down restaurant with a relaxed ambiance called Take a Bao. People are already lined up to order.

We take a seat at a farmhouse table. A waiter comes by with menus.

"We don't need any," says Trina. "Just need popcorn tofu, eight baos, four chicken satay, two duck, and two veggies."

"You got it."

I look at her.

"Trust me."

"Yeah, trust her," says Eric, who can barely fit in his seat.

A second later, Allie walks through the door. She is wearing soccer shorts, and her hair is in a ponytail and scrunchie.

I look at Trina.

She nods at her phone. I smile.

Allie sits next to me. I move over nervously.

"Not a baller?" I ask.

"No, I prefer soccer," she says. "How long are you here for?"

"Just a few weeks," I say.

"I'm training him," Trina jokes. "Right, nephew?"

"Sure, Masi," I say, laughing.

Allie smells like vanilla and bubble gum.

"Are you from LA?" I ask.

"No, actually, I was born in Texas. I came here when I was two."

"Funny, I was born here and left for Orlando at the same age."

"That's crazy," she says, adjusting her napkin on her lap.

We both laugh.

"You're coming to the sneaker drop, right?" Trina asks Allie.

"For sure. Henry is obsessed with those."

"He's gonna be there, eh?" Eric asks.

"Yeah, he's gonna be near there filming a video."

"Who's Henry?" I ask.

"Oh, just a friend," she says. "You might know him. He goes by the handle @thehoophandler. He does all the trick videos."

Trina and Eric shrug and shake their heads.

Just a friend? I didn't like the sound of that. Yeah, I knew about him. He was another hoops influencer who just dribbled the ball, and that's it. He couldn't shoot or score. He did dribble tricks. But he has over a hundred thousand followers.

"Yeah, maybe," I say, trying to be cool.

I drop my fork, and it lands with a metallic bang.

Our food arrives. The waiter brings this incredible fried tofu battered with panko crumbs. We dip it in mint sauce. They bring us chopsticks too.

To be honest, I hate using chopsticks because I never properly learned to use them, so I always defaulted to a fork. Mom and Dad tried teaching me a few times when we went to P.F. Chang's. I refused.

All three rip the paper off and grab one of the tofu pieces. I reluctantly take the wrapper off mine and split the sticks in two.

I watch the three for a moment, trying to mimic them. I go in and grab one. I squeeze too hard, and the tofu piece flies across the table.

The three of them laugh.

"Don't worry, I have the same problem," Allie says.

It makes me feel a little better but still embarrassed. Not Payton embarrassed, though.

"Watch me," she says, gripping one of the sticks. "Pinch it and grip it like a pen."

She inserts the other stick between her thumb and pointer.

"Slide it in between. Easy to squeeze and pick up things. Like this."

She grabs tofu, dips, and eats.

She is a beautiful eater.

"You try."

I take my shot. I grab the tofu, and I'm about to dip it. The piece again pops out and flies across the table.

They all laugh. My cheeks flush, and I can feel myself covering my face with my hands. I'm beginning to feel that compulsion to run away or curl up on the floor, but I feel a gentle hand on my back. It's Allie.

"Dude, relax," she says, giving me a little squeeze on my arm. "We're laughing with you. Not at you. Let's try again. I have a technique. The third time's the charm," she says, smiling.

I take a deep breath and relax. I need to stop overreacting. Trina and Eric both act like nothing is out of the ordinary.

Allie grabs another set of chopsticks. She also pulls her hair band from her ponytail.

She takes the sticks out of the paper holder. She splits them apart and ties her hair band around the end of the sticks. I'm staring in awe.

Then she rips off a third of the paper holder and rolls and folds it. She then takes the piece of paper and slides it through the open end of the chopsticks. The chopsticks stay open.

"Ta-da," she says. "Try this. I call it chopstick training wheels. No offense."

None taken. It's an ingenious device.

I take her invention and try plucking another piece. This time it works. I smile and pop the tofu into my mouth. It's delish. Allie rubs my shoulder playfully. I can't help but bow my head. Everyone claps their hands and cheers me on.

"Raam, it took me a whole week to learn," Trina admits.

Now, I don't feel so bad.

KICKING IT

Neela Kaki points to the dining table, where an assembly line of cardboard boxes sits in front of us in the dining room.

"Your choice," she says, her smile slowly returning. "Well, honestly, you don't have a choice whether you accept this mission or not."

She laughs at her own joke, but her forehead remains as smooth as a baby.

"We . . . meaning you both, have to make this bhusu mix for the wedding. We have four hundred bags we need to fill."

Trina and I look at each other flummoxed.

"What's bhusu?" I ask.

"It's a spicy trail mix that comes from our hometown of Nadiad," Kaki explains. "Your mom knows it very well. I don't think your dad could handle the heat the last time he tasted it. We are giving it to guests during the wedding as a snack."

"Mom, you realize this isn't my wedding?"

"Soon enough, Trina." She grins.

"Ew, Mom," Trina says like someone forced her to eat a cricket.

"I'm joking."

"Can you drop us in Westwood, please?" Trina asks. "We'll be late for this sneaker drop."

"I can take you after you finish your task."

I try lifting one of the boxes onto the table.

"Come on." Trina hops up and down, shaking her head.

"Everyone needs to contribute," Kaki says. "Roll your sleeves, and let's get to business."

Trina throws up her arms in surrender.

Kaki opens the boxes and pulls out an assortment of snacks in different bags ranging from sunflowers and fennel seeds to cashews, peanuts, and more.

She demonstrates the mixing and wrapping process by taking a little of each ingredient, starting with peanuts, and puts it together. She shakes the bag and ties a bow around it.

"Voilà!" she says with glee.

Trina and I split responsibilities. She'll put the first batch of ingredients in, and I'll do the rest and tie the bow. Tag team back again.

We try our first attempts. Kaki insists she must examine our work.

"Way too many chickpeas," she says, tasting it. "Try again."

Trina and I both throw our hands up in mock disbelief.

Kaki demands perfection like she's some judge on a food show competition.

I sample the flavor of the bhusu on my fingertips. Not bad.

"Let me try it," I ask.

"I don't think that's a good idea, beta," Kaki warns me.

I need to flex my Guju-food bona fides. I have better tolerance than my old man.

I take a sample and toss it in my mouth. My tongue feels like someone put a steaming branding iron on it. I run to the kitchen and get a glass of water from the sink. The flames continue to rise, and I'm halfway to spewing fire like a dragon.

Kaki and Trina laugh.

"Have some milk," Trina says. "It helps."

I crack open the fridge and swig the milk right from the gallon. Still blazing. I drain all of it.

Finally, the embers calm down, and my mouth feels charred.

"Just like your dad," Kaki says mockingly. "Can't handle the spice."

Trina pops it in her mouth like popcorn.

I look at her like she's a different species.

"What?" she says. "I thought you called yourself Spicy Curry."

She meant it as a joke, but it reminded me of my fallout with Cake.

Trina and I get back on track, and Kaki approves our third attempt.

Trina and I make a solid team, and we crush all four hundred bags in two hours.

We put everything in a stack of boxes.

Kaki comes back and claps joyfully.

"Nice work! The floral arrangements are coming later today."

"Mom!" Trina exasperates.

"I'm kidding," Kaki says, putting a box into the corner. "Yes, of course, we can do this tomorrow. I also have to pick up some fabric from the India store . . . by the way, who is dropping you home?"

Trina reminds her. "Eric's dad will drop us back."

"Okay, don't be too late."

I can still feel the bhusu burning through my mouth like a hellscape. I just hope they don't tell my dad that I couldn't handle it.

We drive to Westwood and the UCLA campus. Kaki takes us through the hills and the canyons with epic views and curves. For a moment, my head gets nauseous from vertigo.

We finally turn into the campus, which feels empty because of summer. The place is pristine and filled with palm trees, Romanesque buildings, ice cream, and coffee shops.

"You know you were born there," Kaki says while I stare out the window. "We met you there for the first time."

I notice the hospital: Ronald Reagan UCLA Medical Center, a series of modern buildings with travertine panels and large canopies.

"Beyoncé and Jay-Z had their twins there too," Trina chimes in.

"Your mom had a C-section," Kaki says. "She was there for three full days, and you were so small."

"He still is," Trina jokes.

She pinches my cheek, and I turn away.

"Did you know you are in the epicenter of college basketball?"

"Wooden, Jabbar, Walton, Westbrook. It's crazy," I say.

"So, what time will you be back?" Kaki asks Trina. "And are you sure you will be safe? These sneaker drops are dangerous."

"Mom, there's going to be security there. Plus, Eric's dad's going to be with us," Trina says.

"Okay. Keep me posted," Auntie says.

"Can you drop us here?" Trina says as we pass by the Hammer Museum.

"You sure?"

"Yes. I'll give Raam a quick tour before we go to the store."

We get out at a light.

"Please call me as soon as you leave."

"Will do," Trina says as we close the door and hop out.

"Thought this would be fun to give you the full college experience."

I remember Dad taking me to Gainesville. This is different. This is home.

We check out Pauley Pavilion with its blue and gold and see the retired numbers from Bill Walton to Reggie Miller to Lew Alcindor, known as Kareem Abdul-Jabbar. At the bookstore, I pick up a John Wooden biography.

As we walk around campus, I can't help but feel like I'm in some sort of heaven for basketball. The weather doesn't hurt, either.

"Mom told me your mom went to classes here," Trina says.

"Really? I didn't know that," I say.

I always imagined my mom acting or performing. I never knew she attended lectures.

We walk toward a botanical garden, and for the next hour, we walk along a path and take in all the fauna, greenery, and flowers.

"I love walking here," Trina says. "It feels so tranquil."

For the first time, I see her slow down and inhale the world around her and not sprint to the next activity.

I don't doubt how she feels.

Once we're done, we cross a few streets and end up in a long line that extends around the block. They've even set up stanchions like it's a line to some exclusive concert.

Tents are set up, and people sit in camping chairs. It's mostly guys in their twenties and thirties with book bags and baseball caps. I don't see any s'mores or campfires.

"I didn't think the line would be this long right now," Trina says.

She takes her phone out and sends a text. A second later, I hear a ding.

"Looks like Eric is up there. I think he camped here last night," she says, scanning the crowd.

"No way, just for sneakers?" I ask. "Can't you reserve a pair with an app?"

"Dude, these are the XJ 93s off-whites," she says. "There is no bigger sneaker drop this summer."

We walk half a block more, and we see Eric. He's sleeping on a chair with a canned energy drink next to him. Poor guy looks zonked.

Trina shakes him. He shakes his cobwebs from his slumber and stirs awake.

"Is it six p.m. yet?" he asks groggily. "They open the shop?"

"No, not yet. How long have you been here?"

He checks his watch.

"I got here last night. My dad just left."

I notice he has a wristband on his hand and two crumpled bags of McDonald's near his feet.

"How long is the line?"

"Stretches down like two blocks at least."

"Sheesh," Eric says. I can tell he's exhausted.

We timed it right because they might be opening in the next hour. We babysit Eric's place as he goes to the bathroom finally and returns.

We are still in the middle of the queue even though Eric's been here for what feels like days.

Eric tells me the sneaker shop Soul Collective is legendary in LA. It is blacked out with brown wax paper blocking out the windows. Two burly security guards stand in front of the entrance.

The crowd stirs. Police cars drive by, and curious onlookers stare as they pass.

Another hour goes by. The sun has dipped below the sky, and

the red and orange colors of the clouds mix, forming this sublime mélange.

My feet get tired. We take turns sitting in the camping chair.

"I'm hungry," I say.

Trina digs in her bag and gives me some of the bhusu.

I look at her, annoyed.

"Dude, that's all I have."

I pour some into my hands and eat it as fast as possible. My mouth is burning. I take a swig of water.

Why do I subject myself to this?

"Hey, peeps," says a familiar and sweet voice behind me.

Allie smiles at me as she catches up. She's wearing a Rams shirt and jeans. I'm a Bucs fan, but I don't mind.

"Hi, Allie, you finally made it," Trina says.

I forgot she was coming. Not that I have any complaints.

"Is Henry here?" Eric asks.

"He said he might be," she says.

I hope he isn't. I don't know Henry, but I don't like Henry already.

"Hey, Raam, how's it going?" she asks me.

"I'm good," I say.

I'm nervous and start scraping a piece of gum on the ground.

"Heard you're playing in the Ballerfest tournament," she says.

"Who said that?" I ask.

I arch my eyebrows at Trina. There's still no way I'm playing in this tournament.

"He's still figuring it out," Trina says.

"Um, I'm not. I already told you," my voice shrieks.

Trina ignores me. She redoes her hair.

"Any news on the callback?" she asks Allie.

"Actually, yeah," she says, looking down and up with a smile. "I got it."

She yelps, and Trina and she scream together in joy. They both grab each other's hands and jump around. Trina hugs her, and so does Eric.

Allie even hugs me. I don't want to let go.

"We start filming at the end of the summer," she says. "It's a cable show and has already been greenlit for the season."

I don't know what that means, but it sounds exciting.

Mom talked about her Bollywood shoots and how they would film in random buildings, including an air-conditioning factory. I didn't pay much attention to her stories, but I might now.

Finally, we hear through the crowd the store has opened. There's a collective cheer that passes like a wave.

As we slowly roll up, I hear a loud voice bellow from across the street.

"Allie, yo, Allie." The voice belongs to a tall guy with slicked hair pulled back in a man bun. He looks like he's sixteen or something. It's Henry, and he has a crew of friends with him who all look like generic members of a boy band. A *really* annoying boy band.

He hugs her. She doesn't look very excited to see him.

All his friends look like they finished golfing at a country club.

"These are my friends Trina and Eric and Raam," Allie says to Henry.

He nods but doesn't even shake Eric's hand when he reaches out. He doesn't even introduce us to his friends.

"We met a few times," Eric says.

"Yeah, I don't remember," Henry says dismissively.

Henry looks at me with a double take.

"Ayo, are you that kid who Payton posterized?"

I don't answer for a second, but he confirms his answer with my silence.

"Oh, man, you are," he says, cracking up, and hits one of his friends on the shoulder, who also starts laughing.

The gum sticks to my shoe, and my fists clench.

"Must suck to be you," he says smugly. "I wouldn't have the guts to show my face. But hey, we all need to escape."

Allie looks stunned and embarrassed. I look the other way, doing my best to ignore him.

Eric taps me on the back.

"Lines moving, let's go," he says, bypassing Henry and his friends.

Henry walks along with us. When we are near the entrance, he sees the security guard. He greets him like an old friend. They exchange a couple of words, dap, and I see a wad of cash exchanged. He slips through the entire group with his friends.

"Where are you going?" Allie asks.

"Oh, we got a hookup," Henry says.

"Can I go with you?" Eric asks.

"Sorry, man." Henry shrugs his shoulders.

After about ten minutes, Eric gets a chance to finally go inside.

We sit on a curb near the sidewalk, waiting for him.

Henry and his boys walk out with large plastic bags filled with sneaker boxes.

"Man, I can't wait to flip these online," he says. "Gonna put them on the IG, and they will sell quickly."

Henry shows the sneakers to his friends while Allie looks annoyed.

A few moments later, Eric walks out with nothing. His face is boiling with anger.

"They sold out of my size," he says.

"What's your size, Eric?" Trina says.

Trina walks over to Henry. She's not happy. I haven't seen her this mad before as she stomps toward them.

"Hey, guys, do you have a size eleven?" Trina asks. "Eric didn't get a pair because they sold out. He's been waiting for the whole day."

"Oh man, I'm sorry, I can't. I'm saving these," Henry says condescendingly.

Part of me wants to grab a shoe and knock that dude out, and I don't even know him.

"Yo, our ride is on the way. Let's dip," Henry's friend says.

We see a car parked, and someone waves. They barely look at us.

They cross the street, and we are out of luck.

"Sorry," Allie says, "he can be such a selfish turd."

She touches my shoulder gently.

Eric doesn't say anything.

The car horn blares.

"You coming, Allie?"

"Yeah," she says, looking back at us once more. "His parents are giving us a ride."

She leaves. I can see she genuinely feels terrible. Or at least, I hope.

Trina looks over at Eric sympathetically. I can see her chewing her lip.

"Those guys just want to flip that sneaker. I wanted to wear it."

It's around 10 p.m. now, and Eric texts his dad.

A few minutes later, he picks us up.

His dad looks like him but bigger and grayer.

"Any luck?" he asks.

Eric shakes his head.

"No, they were sold out," he says, lowering his head.

"Sorry, man," his dad says. He pats his son on the shoulder and says hello to us.

I find out he's an entertainment lawyer.

"I do copyright for all those YouTube influencers," he mentions. "Not the flashiest of jobs, but it pays the bills."

I try to listen to him tell stories, but my mind goes blurry.

Eric is silent for the rest of the drive home. And I zone out. The roads feel dark and scary. The howls of the coyotes can be heard in the distance.

ROSES AND CANDLES

There's nothing more productive to burn off a night of disappointment than a couple of days of hard-core training.

It's not fun, but Trina's enthusiasm for training is contagious. And waking up at 4 a.m. isn't as bad. Yeah, right. It's pure torture. Trina is insane, and I wonder if Kobe's teammates also thought of him that way.

At first, we do the traditional basketball routines, running, shooting, dribbling, and stretching. Then it changes. Trina tied my right hand behind my back with duct tape, so my left hand was all I could use. I felt like an escaped hostage. It was hard to eat, cut meals, and wipe.

Her rationale was that a former NBA point guard did it, which helped improve his weak hand.

Then we started hiking through Malibu hills and trails, leaving me with blisters and calves that feel like rocks. After comes meditation and yoga. I can only take so many poses of animals and corpses. Mom would laugh because she insists that Americans have been stealing India's contributions, including yoga, chai, and namaste.

At least today, we are in an actual training gym. Eric's parents gave us their pass to the one they use. They have ski and rowing machines, bikes, and treadmills. I've just finished doing lunges and slam balls, and worst of all, bear crawls.

I'm breathing hard, exhausted, ready to faint, and I've collapsed on the floor to catch air.

Trina teaches me the technique of breathing in like I'm smelling a rose and breathing out like I'm blowing out candles on a cake. I wanted to tell her I'm sick of cakes.

I stare at the ceiling, shaped like a martian landscape with its black cratered texture. I hear footsteps just as I'm about to put a cold, wet towel over my head. Trina and Eric hover over me. They are sweating as well and drying themselves off.

Trina takes a swig of water from a bottle. While I gasp, they inhale and exhale like fish underwater.

"You ready for Ballerfest?" Eric asks.

I put my towel back on my face. They've been bugging me to play. I don't understand why they don't find someone else.

"Next week is registration," Trina says.

"Told you," I say. "I'm a no."

Yes, I've been practicing with them, and they're good. Better than me. But mentally, I'm not even close to playing in public or in front of everyone.

"Come on, we have a great squad, and you can give us the outside shooting we need," Eric says.

"I doubt it," I say. It's cool to shoot around, but I'm not risking full-on embarrassment again.

I also realize it'll be hard to find the same chemistry on the court I had with Cake. We were the Spice Brothers, and now we've broken up like Shaq and Kobe.

I can still sense them above me. I want to zone out. My feet are killing me, and my arms feel like they can't move.

I take the towel off my eyes and crouch to my knees.

"All right, at least come with us to ball tomorrow," Eric says.

"I got something special planned. We won't bother you again if you decide you want to play or not play after that."

I take a deep breath. These peeps are relentless.

I nod my head.

"Okay. Fine."

I put my head back down and put a towel over my face. Again, roses and candles.

Uncle drops Trina and me at Venice Beach the following day. We had already walked the Santa Monica Pier and sifted through the Malibu sand. Venice is new territory.

We walk through the famous boardwalk with its wild spectacle of skateboarders, bodybuilders, and street performers. I'm ready to take a dip in the ocean and try surfing when Trina tells me we're not here to lie on the sand or ride the waves. We're here to ball.

"Eric's going to meet us here."

We walk past the skate parks, cafés, and food trucks.

"You know this is one of the meccas for streetball. You ball out here, you can do it anywhere," Trina says proudly. "Your boy Aron and Kobe both played here during summers."

"Yeah, I know," I say.

I'm not sure where we are going to play. The four blue courts are crowded, and every area has a standing-room-only crowd. A giant billboard for the Ballerfest Tournament can be seen across the street. Trina sees me looking at it and smiles. I look away.

My answer is still a definitive no.

"There's a high school game we're gonna crash," she says. "Do me a favor. Pretend you know nothing about basketball. Eric will be there. Also, act like you don't know him. Here," she says, handing me a cap. "Wear these. Hopefully, no one will recognize you."

It's a baseball cap. And goggles. I try them on. I look ridiculous.

I feel like we will be acting in a bad Uncle Drew skit.

Trina looks at me and laughs.

"Mini-Kareem," she says as she dons a large fishing hat that barely fits her head.

We walk over to the crowded area that's got multiple half-court games going on. Palm trees wave back and forth, and the ocean glitters in the background.

When Trina gets there, she starts taking bizarre, weird shots like she has no idea what she's doing. Some of the kids start laughing.

I spot Eric, and he's talking to a group of kids. They are bantering back and forth.

"Man, I could take any two chumps here and win," he says, pointing all over and eyeing us, so their vision focuses on us. The guy knows how to act a part.

The one guy he is directly talking to looks a little older. Maybe in college. He's about the same size as Eric and has a full James Harden beard. He wears an Aron jersey.

"Okay, bro, I'll take you up on that," he says.

He points to us.

"Take the little girl and James Not Worthy, and let's go."

"Dude, I mean real players," Eric says.

"Nah, kid. You said any two. And I'm picking those two."

He emphasizes us. Eric slams the ball in mock anger.

"Ah, fine. You two scrubs, come over here."

Trina prods me.

"Play the part."

"Okay."

We walk over like we are playing nerd stereotypes for an improv play. I'm not a thespian at all, unlike Mom or Allie.

"You two are on my team," he says, motioning in our direction.

"You mean us?" Trina asks, hamming it up. "Great. Awesome."

She should stick to hoops and not act.

"I can't believe we are playing with LeBron," she says.

The crowd begins to gather around the court and starts cracking up. Wannabe James Harden brings his motley crew over, and they size us up. They can't hold back their laughter.

Eric checks the ball into me. These goggles are uncomfortable and sweaty, and my eyes fog up. I pretend to chuck a lousy shot. The ball hits off the backboard and misses badly.

Eric walks over to me.

"Acting part is over. Time to ball."

I nod my head. Trina tosses her hat off and ties her hair into a ponytail.

We get the ball back on a rebound. Trina passes it to me, and I return it to her. She morphs into the Trina I know and schools her defender on a crossover and lobs it over to Eric for the dunk.

These two appear to have developed this act, and I'm watching it all go down. I finally make my contribution by drilling a three.

One of the guys starts talking trash to Trina, and she nutmegs the ball through his legs and goes in for the layup.

"You don't want that smoke," she says, wagging her finger.

The crowd size increases in numbers and intensity. They start getting behind us, oohing and aahing and jeering and cheering. It's like we have our own fan section. Unlike that time at camp, this feels like people are rooting for us, and it feels good. The angrier Harden Beard gets, the more Eric smiles, and the crowd starts ragging him.

We play like a team, one with chemistry and rhythm. We are in sync. We win easily.

Now Eric begins to talk.

"Time to take your lunch and go home," he says.

The guy looks at us, shaking his head, while the crowd heckles him. They start clapping for us after it's over. I can see people recording with their phones. Some of them even pat me on the back as we rest.

Trina smiles, and so do I.

"The old chump hustle," Eric says. "Helps when you two dress like tourists."

We all laugh.

"So, what did we win?" I ask.

"Nothing, bro," Eric says, draining his Gatorade. "Nothing like playing the game and winning. And hearing the crowd cheer for you."

Trina nods her head in agreement.

SARI, NOT SORRY

I haven't worn Indian clothes since Mom had me dance at the Diwali Show at the temple last year. I only did so because Reena was in our group, and the opportunity to be in her presence was worth the sacrifice of having to deal with Mom as the choreographer. I did get jealous of Cake because he was Reena's dance partner.

The blue kurta I'm wearing now itches my back, and I keep trying to scratch it. I envy Bean because he has someone who can scratch his ears.

Today is the Indian wedding day for Sunil and Swati, two people I've never met.

This present garb doesn't belong to me. Kaki asked me to don traditional attire. I didn't bring any Indian clothing from Florida.

Auntie procured this outfit from one of her friends who had old hand-me-downs left because their kid was in college and had outgrown it.

The kurta is also way too big, and whoever was the previous tenant must have been at least six feet tall. I don't know why everyone insists on giving me clothing for a large-size adult.

I look in the mirror and gel my hair back. Yo, at least I'm looking like a maharaja. I head out.

I almost bump into Trina, wearing a gold-and-purple sari. She's even put makeup on. I had never seen her dressed like this. I'm caught off guard. Her curly coils have been straightened.

Bean sneaks up and starts sniffing me.

I stare for a second.

"What?" she says. "I did my hair."

"Nothing. Don't see you in Indian clothes that often."

"I can do baller and Bollywood simultaneously," she says, faking a shot and doing a twirl.

She even grabs a matching clutch. Her fingernails and toenails are painted purple and gold to match her outfit.

"Like the color scheme?" she asks.

"Dope," I say, nodding my head.

"Are you two ready?" Auntie yells from the door. "I don't want to be late. Your dad is in the car already."

"Mom, we have two hours before the wedding starts," Trina says.

"This is LA, and I'm not taking a chance with traffic. We have to go all the way to Laguna Beach."

We walk over to the door. Auntie gives us a once-over. She looks at me.

"Mom, you can smile," Trina says.

Kaki playfully smacks her shoulder.

"Let me send your mom a picture."

She takes a photo with her camera.

She also looks at Trina.

"You look like a maharani, my dear," she says. "You forgot your bindi."

Trina blushes, something I notice for the first time.

She rummages in her purse, finds a packet, and sticks it on Trina's forehead.

"Thanks, Mom."

She looks over the house one more time.

"Looks like we got everything."

The night before, we hauled boxes of decorations, flowers, and sweets for the wedding to the car.

"Mom, we're good."

"Can you drop Bean next door?" Auntie asks. "Ms. Ela is watching him."

Bean's ears perk up.

"Ms. Ela has a pug named Adele that Bean is fond of," Trina says.

When we arrive in the parking garage, Uncle watches a cricket match on his phone. We can't even see outside the back of the car because the boxes are stacked with snack mix and pizza cutters.

Uncle looks annoyed he's being interrupted.

"Kohli is at bat," he says.

Kaki clucks her tongue at him.

"Drive," she demands.

He sighs and starts the car.

"After this, I can get my house back."

Kaki nudges him.

The drive is boring as we drive through industrial parks and the cityscapes, but it becomes scenic once we get off the 405 highway. There are harbors, sailboats, and candle shops along the waterfront. That's the crazy thing about LA. Drive in any direction for thirty minutes, and you are in a different climate and topography.

Trina points to another area across a bridge that looks like a village of shops.

"That's Balboa Island. They have frozen bananas. So good."

We finally get to our destination. It's a Hyatt Resort right on the beach.

I'd been to a couple of weddings in Orlando. Still, they were usually held at the temple, and the reception was at the hotel ballroom on International Drive. Usually, one is owned by Vipul Uncle.

Dad filmed many of the weddings, but he hated it. However, this location is one even he'd be excited by.

We park. As we walk toward the entrance, I hear the baraat has already begun. We are on the groom's side, so we join a sizable group of uniformed band members playing dhols, tuba, and trumpet, and a gaggle of sweaty uncles, gyrating aunties, and crying babies.

They move in front of the groom, who sits on top of a painted elephant. I'd seen horses and carriages, but this was something new. The non-wedding hotel guests stare at it like those scientists in *Jurassic Park* did the first time they whisked off their sunglasses, mouths ajar, at the Brachiosaurus.

Trina tells me the groom's side is loaded. Even for Newport, this is an extravagant gala.

The group moves from the parking lot toward the hotel.

We join in. Trina and I don't know anyone, so we just watch and clap along.

Mom would throw me into the ring.

Two drones hover and buzz above us.

Kaki is lost in the shuffle, and Uncle takes his phone out and grabs some snaps of all the wedding guests.

The beat increases, and finally, we meet the bride's side near the entrance. I feel bad for one non-wedding family as they try to squeeze through the double doors.

The weather is excellent, and the palms sway back and forth. I can smell the ocean too.

Trina and I head inside and then outside. The wedding is held on the lawn outdoors, stretching to the beach. It's a picturesque setting.

The chairs are spread out on the white sand, and a giant mandap is set up, decorated in flowers and ornate fabrics.

They pass out sun umbrellas to protect everyone from the heat.

There's an area for chai and water, and on the chairs are all the bags we packed of bhusu. Someone must have grabbed them from the car.

"They can plan a million-dollar wedding, yet us kids have to do manual labor," Trina says.

Trina grabs a bag and gestures if I want any.

"I've had my share," I say. "My mouth is still burning."

"Wuss," she says, bumping my shoulder.

We take a seat in the back.

A few minutes later, the crowd settles in, and the bride comes through on a palanquin held by four guys. The carriage is adorned with flowers and ornate mehndi. I'd never seen something so lavish and regal.

The wedding starts and the bride and groom have a sheet separating them while the priest performs the Sanskrit blessing.

A camera crew is set up in all directions recording everything. It all looks like a postcard I can send to Mom and Dad.

Once the wedding rituals kick off, Trina and I get bored. We stare at the four-page booklet they provided that explains every ritual. These things could go on for a while.

An hour later, it surprisingly concludes after the bride and groom go around in circles and sit down. We all clap, more for relief.

"That's the fastest I've ever seen one of these done," I say.

"Me too," Trina says as we get up and stretch our legs.

We run into Uncle and Kaki.

Uncle looks exhausted. Kaki looks like she can do another two rounds.

"You guys can go explore and come back for the cocktail hour. It starts in two hours," Kaki says.

"Great. Let's go."

Trina and I are off.

The resort stretches for acres. We walk through the gallery of shops inside the hotel. We see uncles at the bar and aunties talking on benches. All the non-wedding guests stare at us like we are animals in a zoo.

We check out the shops, food court, and gym. They have an atrium area where parrots and other birds hang out. We feed some of them.

We finally walk back outside toward the tennis courts and volleyball area. Then we see it—a full outdoor court near the beach.

A closer look, and we can see three people shooting baskets. And they look like us in Indian garb.

Trina and I walk toward them until she abruptly turns around.

"Let's go somewhere else," she says.

"Why? We can ball on the beach."

I can see her face cringe.

A loud yell bellows from the court. The guys approach.

"Oh, look, it's Trina wannabe baller," one of the guys says. "I couldn't recognize you. You are dressed as a girl."

Three Indian guys with spiked haircuts and rattails approach us. They could be villains from a Bollywood movie.

They seem to know Trina and are already upsetting me.

Trina rolls her eyes.

I walk over to the guy.

"Do we have a problem, Trina?" I ask. "Who are these fools?"

"Meet Tapan Sukheja and his cousins, Navin and Nilesh. If you wonder about that stinky stench, it comes from them."

Tapan is as tall as Eric but burlier. He looks a few years older.

"Who is this, your bodyguard?" he says.

"Cousin."

"You got a problem, dude?" I say.

"It's been a while, Tapan. Are you still licking your chops since I beat you?"

"I had a sprained ankle."

"Excuses," Trina says.

She doesn't back down to anyone.

"I can take you anytime. You got lucky."

"No better time than the present," she says firmly. "We won't need a camp this time. I can do it again, even with a sari."

The guys and I look at her, shocked. It's one thing to face someone at a camp, but to challenge a dude who is double your height, wearing a sari and heels?

Trina carries herself with courage; I envy her.

Tapan's boys urge him on.

Trina grabs the ball from him and walks over to the court. We all follow.

She bounces the ball on the court, takes off her heels and clutch. She's going to play with her bare feet. My cuz is cray cray.

"Trina, you think this is a good idea?" I ask. She even painted her toenails.

"I got this, cuz," she says, chucking her heels into the sand.

She ties her pallu into the petticoat portion of her sari.

Tapan wears a dress jacket and slacks. He rolls up his sleeves.

"Play to five. I hit this. My ball."

She takes one dribble and drains the shot—all net.

"Check," she says, sending the ball to Tapan's chest. He sends it back and tries to cover her defense.

He tries to body her, but she is too quick and drives quickly to the net for an easy lay-in. But when she lands, I can see her cringe a little.

I'm not sure how she's playing with no shoes.

She gets the ball back and hits a midrange j: 2–0.

"Sari, not sorry," she yells with a smirk.

This is going to get embarrassing. And I love every moment of it. I wish I had some popcorn.

Tapan gets overaggressive.

"Lucky. You can't play with the boys, so stick to your little girl's side."

Trina doesn't even look at him.

Tapan tries to rile her up as he throws the ball away from her. I grab it and throw it back.

Trina winks at me.

"Watch."

She takes the ball back to the key.

Tapan comes up to cover her. Trina backs away, uses a quick hesitation, and crosses him up. Tapan falls to the ground. Trina steps back and arcs a rainbow three. The ball falls into the net like a raindrop into a bucket. She keeps her wrist up and waves at Tapan, who tries to get up.

"So purdy."

She slips on her heels and throws the clutch on her shoulder. Not a strand of hair out of place.

"How's my makeup?" she says, rubbing her lip.

"Great, not a blemish," I say.

She glares at Tapan and his friends, who look at her, stunned.

"Soft like Charmin," she says, tossing the ball to him.

I don't even know what to say.

"Did you just drop that Kobe line?"

"Yup, remember, Raam, I didn't start it. I finished it."

We make it back for the cocktail party, where we devour a buffet of chicken tikka masala, lamb kebabs, and more.

Trina and I do a dope improv bhangra dance step at the reception. One that would make Mom smile. Kaki ends up getting it on her phone and sending it to her. We have a great time. We don't see Tapan the entire night. The dude probably got swept away in the ocean.

On the way back to the car, Trina's face winces. I can see she's favoring her knee.

"You okay?" I ask.

I can see her cringe as we sit in the back.

"I'm fine," she says, smiling. "I hate heels. Must have tweaked it while we were dancing."

SATI SHAVES HER HEAD

Uncle and Kaki, Trina, and I play board games and finish a LEGO® *Star Wars* battleship project. I go to the kitchen and grab water. Bean follows me like he always does. I don't mind at all.

I pick up a tennis ball and throw it into the living room toward a bookshelf.

Bean, of course, wants me to chase him, so I walk over. As I do, I feel this rumble, and the entire house starts to shake like we're in a snow globe. Dishes rattle in the kitchen. The ceiling fan looks like it's going to spin out. The board game pieces fall to the ground.

"Is that a . . ." I ask.

"Yeah, genius. Earthquake!" Trina yells, and all of us scamper under the large dining table and duck underneath it.

Books and DVDs fall off the shelf, and I can hear a glass shatter in the kitchen.

The shaking feels like minutes, but it lasts for only fifteen seconds.

We wait five minutes before we get up.

I'm still shaking. No pun intended.

Mahendra Uncle puts his hand on my shoulder to calm me down.

"You okay, Raam?" he asks. "That wasn't that bad compared to the one we had in '94."

"Dude, that was a baby," Trina says, smirking.

Kaki is already sweeping up the broken glass in the kitchen.

"I've been through a hurricane before, and I'd do that ten more times before I want to experience another earthquake," I say.

It's true. I'll take 150 mph winds and rain. At least you can plan for a hurricane.

They all laugh.

"Help me with this stuff," Trina says, pointing to the books and DVDs that fell off the shelf.

I help her pick up the items, random bestsellers, and

classics, and see some DVDs. There is one distinct, familiar red cover. I nearly drop it when I spot the title. It's *Sati Shaves Her Head*. The exact image of the movie poster I found in the garage.

I bring it back to the living area, frazzled.

I show it to Uncle and Kaki. They look at it bemused like it's an old photograph.

"Oh, I remember this," Uncle says while putting a lamp back up. "We went to the premiere in Hollywood."

"Wasn't it at the New Beverly, the theater that Tarantino owns?" Kaki asks, arching an eyebrow.

"Indeed," Uncle says. "Pretty good film. I honestly was surprised."

"Your parents gave us a copy," Kaki says as she throws away the broken glass into the garbage can.

"I mean, we did help fund it," Uncle jokes.

Trina looks at the back of the case.

"Oh. Can I watch it?" I ask.

They look at each other.

"It's a bit mature."

"Come on, Mom!" Trina says.

We're both giddy.

"Okay, I guess you're old enough," Kaki says.

"I'll warm up some popcorn," I say.

"Wait." Uncle pauses. "Do we have a DVD player?"

"I think I have an old PlayStation around," Trina says.

After a few minutes of digging through random closets, we find the old game system in the laundry area. We hook all the cables up and hope it works. It does.

We all sit to watch. Thankfully, the ground beneath our feet remains stable. No aftershocks or waves.

The movie begins with a house party and people hanging out. It looks like a high school scene. I see Mom make a cameo as an extra dancing in the background. Dad is there too, holding a red cup. The movie focuses on two cousin sisters. One from India and one from America. It's a *Mean Girls*–like story where Nikki, the American cousin, played by Amy Simone, transforms her dopey Indian cousin Sati into the most popular girl in their social circle. However, Nikki gets jealous when Sati wins the heart of the guy who used to like her. And it's strange because the guy's name is Ramanujan. Nikki tricks Sati into shaving her head, but Sati gets the last laugh when she gets her cousin back, in the end, by shaving Nikki's head. I can't help but feel I was named after that character. Also, I can't help but feel like Mom and Sati are similar in their backgrounds.

Some adult cursing and some scenes make me feel uncomfortable in front of Uncle and Kaki. Still, I've seen more graphic stuff on TV.

I text both of my parents after we're done.

ME: **Saw Sati. I liked it.**

DAD: **You're too young to watch that movie.**

ME: **Did you name me after that character Ramanujan?**

MOM: **LOL. Kind of. You were named after the mathematician.**

DAD: **The most famous mathematician. He was a genius and brilliant.**

ME: **Oh. That's cool. Like me.**

MOM: **You have that type of talent.**

ME: **Why are you not making more movies anymore?**

DAD: **A long time ago. Different era.**

ME: **Mom, were you Sati? Why did you guys leave California? You didn't answer last time.**

DAD: **No, she wasn't. Things change. Other things became a priority.**

I wanted Mom to answer the question.

ME: **Did you stop making movies because I was born?**
MOM: **No. We didn't have a great experience making that movie. And we wanted to do other things. And Cali didn't have the same feeling for us after you were born. We were lonely. And, yes, there was a lot to Sati I could relate to.**
DAD: **We had our adventure, and you are having yours. Hope you're having fun.**
ME: **You guys should make another movie. We could team up.**

For some reason, they don't answer. Finally, Mom says good night.

All night, I wondered why my dad kept avoiding the question about leaving Los Angeles and why my mom didn't answer my idea. I also realize I didn't even mention my first earthquake.

I ask Neela Kaki about it while making scrambled eggs.

"Why do you think my parents left LA?" I ask.

She looks tired this morning. Her eyes are red. It's still strange to see her arch her forehead.

"Beta, your parents needed a change," she says, whisking the yolks.

"From what? Because they had me."

Kaki cooks the eggs in the pan, scooping and scraping them up with a spatula.

"No, not at all," she says, laying her hand gently on my cheek.

"Why do you think they didn't make another movie?"

"I don't know, beta," she says as she puts the eggs onto my plate.

I text my parents again that night.

ME: **So u didn't answer my question.**

Mom messages me separately.

MOM: **the experience wasn't one I wanted to live through again. Your dad and I argued a lot on-site.**

ME: **oh.**

MOM: **your dad wants to do another movie, but I don't think I can.**

ME: **are you getting along better?**

MOM: **we are trying. Get some sleep, beta.**

ME: **ok gn.**

MOM: **Jsk sweetie.**

I barely sleep.

ALL-ROUNDER

It's Saturday morning near the end of July, and surprisingly Trina is still asleep as I come downstairs. She's been bugging me to play in Ballerfest, but I'm not feeling it. I can't see myself playing in a tournament like that. Even with the epic scene in Venice, I'm still fearful. The visions of Hoop Con still shadow my thoughts.

Bean comes in for a back-of-the-head rub. He's a big goof. The house is quiet except for the kitchen.

I approach and see Uncle dressed in cricket gear, a sweater vest, and pants. All white. The clothes are snug, but he looks comfortable.

He makes a smoothie at the counter by throwing random powders, spices, and fruits like pomegranates and apples into a blender.

He holds a bunch of red seeds that look like ants.

"Hemani," he says, mustache twitching. "Hm, I think in English they're called garden cress. Very good for the immune system, loaded with protein."

He throws it into a mixer and grinds it into a greenish liquid. He pours it into a giant water bottle.

"Try it," he says, offering me a glass.

I reluctantly do.

I gag. It's disgusting.

Uncle laughs.

"Not for the fainthearted," he says. "What are you doing this morning, Raam?"

"Um, we were gonna practice, but Trina is still asleep. I was up all night."

"Want to practice cricket today?" he asks. "I've got practice this morning. Come. You'll enjoy it. Learn a truly American sport."

I only played cricket when I was in India. Dad preferred baseball.

I'd been in hoops mode since I got here. A change of scenery would be a good thing.

"Sure. Sounds fun," I say. "I don't have a sweater."

"You don't need one."

I figure I'd played Little League and had tennis lessons, so swinging a cricket bat would be easy.

The matches last forever; they drink tea and eat crumpets during breaks. They have batters, but their pitchers are called bowlers.

Uncle and I haven't hung out much since I got here, so this might be a good bonding session.

We get in the car and drive over to Van Nuys. They have an entire cricket facility with multiple fields and practice nets. I have to see this for myself.

It's hard to fathom that Mahendra Uncle is my grandfather's brother. He's a few years older than my dad, but his hair is thicker and darker. Must be the dry air.

"How are you enjoying your trip?" he asks me.

"It's solid. It's different, for sure."

"I always say, 'You could travel the world, but nothing comes close to the golden coast.'"

I'm sure that's Katy Perry, but I will not argue.

We drive through a swath of land in the San Fernando

Valley, twenty minutes northwest of downtown Los Angeles, next to an archery range and a golf course. On a billboard, another sign for the Ballerfest Tournament appears. I try to ignore it.

"You know cricket is the original American pastime?"

"No way."

"Yup, the first international sporting event in the modern world was a cricket match between the United States and Canada in 1844."

I'm impressed by Uncle's knowledge.

"Your dada taught me to play cricket," my uncle says.

"Really?"

"He was an excellent player in his youth. Played for the Gujarat team. His diabetes slowed him down. Otherwise, he was good enough to play for India."

"Maybe I should switch," I joke.

I didn't know my dada as well as I wanted to, and since he passed, I have always wanted to learn more about him.

We park. There are four big cricket fields and several nets that look like batting cages.

I see the Leo Magnus Cricket Complex sign.

Hobby airplanes buzz overhead, and red-tailed hawks swoop down from willow trees.

A man wearing a white panama hat puts on knee guards near the batting nets.

Some players gather in a semicircle and practice fielding drills. Shouts of "Come on, guys, let's go!" echo in English and Hindi.

An ice cream man pushes his jingling cart around the green lawn.

Uncle greets a man in his fifties dressed in whites and stands in a makeshift line, awaiting his turn to bowl to a batter.

"Meet my nephew, Raam," Uncle says.

The man shakes my hand.

"Good day, young man," he says. "Your uncle is a mighty wicketkeeper and a mean bowler."

He says his name is Mark, and he's a pilot from New Zealand who settled in Rancho Cucamonga.

"What position do you play?" I ask.

"Slow-medium left hand over the wicket can swing both ways occasionally," he says.

I have no idea what that means.

Standing in line with him are other immigrants from all over the world.

Uncle's team is called the Corinthians, and they've been around since 1934.

"Frankenstein played for us," Mark tells me. "The actor who played him played for the team."

He's like the team historian. He even tells me they did funerals at this field.

"They played bagpipes," he says.

Uncle lines up to bowl, brings me along, and gives me a quick tutorial.

Run up: Bunny ears around the ball, pull the magic string, and windmill the arm over.

It's way more complicated than pitching, and I throw the ball worse than some celebrities throw botched first pitches.

On my second attempt, I nearly throw out my arm.

"Maybe you are a batsman," Uncle says. "Not an all-arounder."

They are the Ohtani of cricket.

The bat looks like a paddle that I can row with.

I line up in the net and try to attempt the proper stance.

Uncle tosses me a pitch. The ball bounces, and I take a giant swing. I miss it so badly I fall on my butt. Uncle tries not to laugh. But for some reason, I do.

He and his other teammates, all guys ages twenty-five to sixty from India to England, from slim to chubby, all enjoy playing the game for a simple reason. It's fun.

That's something I've missed in basketball.

We end practice with homemade chai and chutney sandwiches, which one of the players' wives made.

Uncle tells me I did a solid job, but I'm horrible. I don't care.

On the walk back to the car, you can hear that sweet thwack of a bat in the distance. It sounds like music.

Later in the evening, Uncle finally gets a chance to use his tandoori grill.

We all go up to the terrace as Uncle dips the fresh naan into the oven and hooks the tandoori chicken and lamb kebabs onto the long skewers. The tangy, spicy aroma permeates the air. I help Trina make some fresh chutney and raita, and we all sit down and watch an immaculate sunset dip over the mountains.

My whole body aches.

"You see why I stick to one sport," Trina says. "By the way," she asks. "Are you still playing hard to get, or are you gonna play with us in Ballerfest?"

"I don't know, Trina," I say.

"We're getting to the last minute," she says, annoyed. I know she's frustrated with me.

"Oh, by the way, Allie dropped by," Trina says to me, changing the subject. "She invited us to her birthday party at Fun 'N' Games. She specifically mentioned you."

Trina winks.

"What's Fun 'N' Games?"

"Awesome new amusement park/arcade that opened up recently. Parties there are epic."

Trina takes a bite of the chicken.

"Dad, this is so good," she says, nodding her head.

"The key is the papaya," he says like a Michelin chef.

I finally try my food, and it's indeed delicious. I haven't had a meal like this in a long time.

REGARDING HENRY

In front of me, the glowing neon sign of Fun 'N' Games shines like a thousand suns. We're in downtown Burbank walking from the parking lot to Allie's birthday party.

I have her gift tucked in my arm. I wrapped it myself. Trina mocks me for the lackluster job I did. I'm no help during Christmastime.

I bought Allie customized chopsticks with her name on them. Trina bought her a Polaroid camera. She gets annoyed when I insist on shaking it.

We meet Eric in front. He's giddy as a schoolkid.

"Dude, last time I was here," he says, hopping up and down, "I won almost five thousand tickets in the Tower of Tickets machine. All I need is one thousand more, and I can get that new PlayStation."

Fun 'N' Games is a giant bonanza of games and amusements, part carnival, part arcade, part sports bar. It features everything you can desire for pure diversion and masti, from mini-golf courses, go-karts, and bumper boats to an open-air arcade with games, including retro favorites like *NBA Jam* and *Mortal Kombat*.

We're given a map when we walk in. That's how big this place is.

The music is loud and complex, and the lights are bright, dizzying, and flashing with enough spark to cause a seizure. Everything glows, from the miniature bowling lanes to the white lights of the prize counter with its giant bears and LEGO® *Star Wars* sets.

It's overwhelming. I've been to places like this, but this area is on steroids.

We're supposed to meet Allie and the rest of the guests near the restaurant area. We swing to our left and head into a seating area with sixty giant TVs broadcasting summer baseball and cornhole.

Allie sits at a table filled with presents and bar food munchies like wings, pizza, and burgers. I can smell the addictive scent of french fries and burned cheese. She's giving away game cards to guests so they can entertain themselves. I miss the old days of coins.

She sees us and smiles.

"Finally," she says.

I hand her the gift.

"You shouldn't have," she says, touching my elbow. I think I blush.

She gives us all hugs and then hands each of us a card.

"We have two hours unlimited. Enjoy your heart out!"

I want to hang with Allie, but I can see she's busy socializing with all her guests. I mean, it is her birthday. And she has to play the host.

Trina, Eric, and I head over to the arcade. I pass by a giant Connect Four machine and air hockey table, turn, and Henry and his crew are standing in front of a game called Loose Change. The game's object is to roll a ball into specific holes with a coin value and get as close to ninety-nine as possible before going over.

Henry takes a long straw and puts it under the glass shield of the machine. One of his friends films with his phone, and the other stands around watching people pass by.

They're cheating.

They collect the main prize. A roll of tickets cranks out of the machine.

Henry sees me.

"What's up, Raam? Get dunked on again?" He laughs.

Really, bro? Can't be more original.

"What are you guys doing?" I ask. I know I sound like a security guard.

"We're filming a video for my channel."

"On cheating?"

"Hacking," he says abruptly.

"Can't win with skill. Don't you think it's wrong?" I cross-examine.

I purposely keep my chin up and hands crossed.

"Why do you care?" he says. "It's none of your business."

"Why not play fairly?"

Henry wanders over to me. I stand my ground.

At this point, Trina and Eric come back.

"All good?" Eric asks, assessing the situation.

He spots Henry and crosses his arms.

"Oh, yo," Henry says, pointing to Eric's sneakers. He's wearing the XJs.

"I see you didn't get yours," he says. "Tough, bro. I flipped the others for a nice profit."

"That's great, man," Eric says, bemused.

"I might have another pair. I could flip those your way but can't do retail price."

"I'm good," Eric says patiently.

For some reason, I'm fed up with Henry and his crew. There are guys like them everywhere. They need to be put in their place, like the Moores. And I'm going to do it now.

"Why don't you play us fair and square here and see who wins?" I say.

They look at one another and laugh.

"Hah. For sure," Henry says. "After destroying you here, we'll do the same at Ballerfest. We heard you are playing?"

I look curiously at Trina but don't say anything.

"So, what's your point?" Trina asks.

"We can take you here and on the court," Henry says.

"Yeah, right," I say. "What do we get when we destroy you?"

"I'll delete the video."

"And you'll stop cheating," I add.

"Winner gets all the tickets," says Eric.

He looks at Eric.

"Heard you bragging that you had five thousand tickets already."

"Again, your point?"

"Heck, since I'm such a good guy," Henry boasts, "I'll even give poor Eric a pair of XJs if you win."

"Fine, let's go. Best of three contests."

Game on, like *Donkey Kong*.

First up is Skee-Ball. We head over, adrenaline running through me.

I am a solid Skee-Baller. At Chuck E. Cheese, I dominated. Now, Henry would face my wrath.

"Please, go first," Henry insists.

Fine with me.

"One game. The highest score wins," I say.

The holes are scored from 100 on down. The key is hitting the 40 each time. It's easy and consistent.

I bend my knees and use my stance. Follow through. Routine. Like a free throw.

I score 400. Solid. This will be hard to beat.

Henry nods his head.

"Wow, pretty impressive."

It is.

He starts. He misses badly in the first ball, and it drains into the 5 points area. A smirk crosses his face like the Joker.

He starts angling the ball on the side of the game like a backboard and racking up 100 points in succession each. It's not luck as he hits eight in a row. He doubles my score.

"Wow, it must be my lucky day," he says.

"That's cheating," I say.

"How?" he asks mockingly. "I just bowled as you did."

He takes out his pockets.

"See, nothing."

I can't argue. He knew how to manipulate the game. I got outstrategized.

"Let's race some go-karts," Eric says, irritated. "Now it's my chance to put this scrub in check."

Henry grins.

Eric puts on his helmet. He takes a seat and revs the engine. Trina and I watch from the side.

The headlights of the cars beam bright.

Eric and Henry stare down each other at the starting line.

And we're off. They are speed demons at Daytona.

Eric takes an early lead, but Henry cuts him off, sending Eric crashing into the cones. Eric reverses out. His face contorts into a rage of anger. When Eric is back on course, Henry is crossing the finish line.

Henry's boys are filming all of it. He has already won all the events so far.

"You know," he says, removing his helmet. "I can just take your tickets now, and you guys can walk on out of here, but since I'm such a nice guy, I'll play you one more time and allow you to win."

"Bring it," Trina says. "I'll handle this myself."

"Oh, feisty." Henry gesticulates wildly. "How about a game of hoops?"

He points to the Pop-A-Shot hoops game.

Trina smiles. This is her strength. She taps her toes and re-adjusts her hair into a bun.

She goes first. When the bell rings, she starts knocking down shots. By the time she's done, she has 40 points.

We are all stoked as we high-five her. That's a challenging score to match. No matter how good Henry thinks he is.

He shrugs his shoulders as he starts.

The balls roll under the mesh guard. Instead of shooting the ball, he picks each ball up and starts firing them under the net like dodgeball.

For some reason, the score keeps increasing. Trina's 40-point score gets demolished, and there are still 15 seconds left.

We have no idea what's happening.

"Now, that's cheating," Trina says.

"Nope," Henry says. "It's called winning. Now hand over your tickets and get out."

We all want to crush the guy and his friends, but a deal is a deal. We give Henry our winnings, including Eric. I feel bad. This is my fault. He looks stunned.

I got outsized and outmatched. Henry tabulates the tickets and laughs.

"I'll say hi to Allie for you," he says, rubbing it in. "And don't forget we'll see each other soon when we whip you on the court."

I don't react. I take a deep breath and let my anger subside. I've been here before, and I'm getting tested again.

"Don't worry," I say. "We'll see you soon."

Eric and Trina are upset. But there's no point in reacting now. That's what Henry wants. This is the Moores and Payton all riling me up. I just smile and leave.

All of us walk out of the building, heads down.

Eric kicks a garbage can in frustration. I can hear him crack his knuckles as his fist clenches.

"Look," I say. "We lost. Simple. Now let's regroup. And get ready for Ballerfest."

"So, you are in?" Trina asks me.

"Was there any doubt?" I say, smiling.

She pushes me playfully and grins. Even Eric cracks up.

There was a lot of doubt, but it's all gone. The choice was always evident. I just didn't see it till now.

HOOP IT UP

It's early August, and the Ballerfest 3-on-3 Tournament is here.

I don't think Trina or I slept last night. She wakes me up and is as exhilarated as Bean is with a tennis ball.

"Look what I got made," she says.

From around her back, she tosses me a customized team jersey. She dubbed us the Raamstars. I'm overwhelmed.

"No way, that's awesome," I say examining it.

She gives me the #33 jersey like Aron. The jersey is dark blue with orange borders and a scary font for the name.

"Well, Eric and I decided you put in a lot of effort. I thought about naming us the Kobeans, but Raamstars is cool. Plus, I dig the *Space Jam* look and feel."

"Me too!"

"You ready?"

"Ready as always."

"How's your knee?" I ask.

She bends her knee slowly.

"I'm walking," she says. "I'm good to go. Let's go win."

Happily, the shirt Trina got for me fits.

I take a deep breath. We eat a quick breakfast of Fruit Loops.

The doorbell rings. Eric is here.

He's wearing his jersey too.

"Yo, this is on fleek!" he says, pinching the sleeves.

We look good now. We have to play well too.

Uncle and Kaki drive us downtown.

It's surreal to be playing at the exact location where Kobe played.

I nudge Trina.

She's smiling too. She wore her hair in a giant ponytail with purple and gold clips.

"It's my first time playing here," she says. "I saw Kobe play here the year he retired. But I'm getting chills."

The tournament is going to be a weekend-long competition.

They advertise it as the "largest 3-on-3 streetball basket-ball tournament on Earth, with over 6,000 teams, 3,000 volunteers, 25,000 fans, and 100 courts spanning 45 city blocks!"

The rules are we play to 15. One point per basket, threes count as 2, and there's even a four-point shot that gives us 3 points. It's a 30-foot Steph-range three. We're allowed to double-team, but no zone.

This is all going down at LA Live, the downtown Los Angeles sports and entertainment district where the Lakers and Clippers play.

We enter the complex, and basketball courts are everywhere between the ESPN studio, the restaurants, and even parking lot areas.

We end up finding parking. We grab our basketballs and head up the escalator.

There's a festival feel everywhere. It feels kinetic. Street per-formers, dance groups, live art, and food surround the courts. Games are being played everywhere. The streets are closed down. Security is ubiquitous, with the Lakers and Clippers arena in the foreground.

A station is set up to showcase Kobe murals. We walk by and pay our respects.

It's emotional to see the Kobe and Gigi paintings. Trina pauses and says a prayer. Eric and I nod our heads respectfully and gently touch the figures for a blessing.

Around us, we see restaurants, the Grammy Museum, and a bowling alley.

There's basketball everywhere. Children, teens, adults, people in wheelchairs, men, and women are all playing.

They set up a giant canopy in one of the parking lots to cover it from the sun. Trina, Eric, and I walk over to the registration desk.

We are in the 11–14 co-ed group and need to play at least four games to win, starting with two qualifying games, then the quarter- and semifinal today.

If we win, the final takes place tomorrow at center court.

Our first opponent is the Lebroniacs.

As we find our first court, I spot a dunk contest. One of the contestants leaps over three kids.

There's a large crowd sitting in makeshift stands. They are all standing. We bob and weave through the crowd, and I hear a familiar voice behind us.

"Wait up, wait up," says Allie, speeding up to us. She's also wearing the Raamstars jersey.

"I was looking for you guys."

"What are you doing here?" I ask, surprised and delighted.

"Cheering you guys on," she says. "I didn't get a chance to see you before you left."

"We had some issues with your friend," Trina says.

"Who, Henry?"

"Yeah," I respond.

"Don't worry, he's in the rearview," she says. "What a selfish dope. He wasn't invited, and he crashed my party and almost ruined it."

"He ruined our time for sure," Eric says.

Regardless, we're happy to see her, and I'm stoked she's cheering for us.

I've never played in front of her before, so I hope I don't screw it up. I can feel my arms tingle.

But I got the tools now to handle what may come.

We get over to the court. It's near the Grammy Museum. Our first opponents are three triplets, and I have nightmares of the Moores magnified.

We take a few shots. Eric is taller than the rest of the players.

Trina talks to us. She's our Coach Pop and Steve Kerr.

"Keep it simple. Let's run motion. Remember, they're playing checkers. We are playing chess."

We put our hands out.

"On three, two, one . . . Raamstars!"

Now all the practice is going to be tested.

We get the ball first.

Trina handles the ball at the key. She wears a new therapeutic cushioned sleeve on her knees. No matter how much I ask her about it, she refuses to acknowledge any pain.

I run up to her and grab the pass and dish it back.

Eric and she set up a pick and roll. It's a game they know, like Cake and I play.

I observe more than participate. It's the perfect seat to watch them shake and bake.

Trina feeds Eric in the post, and he uses a quick drop step in for the lay-in or banks it.

We are playing beautiful basketball, and I get my points in as I hit a deep three and an open j from the baseline. My defense is tight, and I remain pesky.

We send the triplets packing, winning 15–4.

We are elated, and Allie cheers for us as well. She sits with Uncle and Kaki.

I spot Henry. He walks by us when we step off the court to grab a drink.

"Don't think this will be easy," he threatens. "You don't want to face us. I'll make the Fun 'N' Games beating look merciful."

Puh-lease.

Before I can say anything to him, Trina pulls me aside.

"You'll get your moment," she says. "We will get our chance."

There's another hour to go before our next game.

I check our schedule for the next opponent. We're playing a team called the Thuggah Muggahs. We're up next.

The dudes are Filipino and taller than all of us. Even Eric.

I give them props on their team name. PBS representin'!

Trina tells me I'm handling the rock more.

I check the ball to the guy with spiky purple hair.

My first pass to Trina is picked off, resulting in an easy score. I'm dejected. My thoughts keep running back to the past.

Trina puts her arm around my shoulder.

"Take a deep breath."

They miss the next shot. Eric grabs the board and hands it off to Trina. She gives it back to me.

Trina creates enough space between her and her defender, and I dish it to her.

She's a magician with the ball. She always seems to anticipate the action. She pivots, measures precisely where she wants to go, and slices angles like a five-star chef chops ingredients.

She pump-fakes, gets her man up, and drills the jumper.

Bang!

Eric dominated the last game. This one is all Trina.

She uses all parts of the court to score, but her midrange is a thing of beauty.

We win 15–6, and she scores 10.

"That was awesome," I say to her.

She smacks my hand with the hardest five I've ever felt. My palm is red. She feeds off this. She's an adrenaline junkie.

"We win one more game, we play for the championship," she says.

We break for lunch. As I walk, I notice Henry and his team playing their game.

I pause to watch them. I'm shocked. They're legit.

I'd seen Henry's ball handling on social. I thought he was a one-trick pony like many of these Insta-ballers, but he's decent. He and his team are more physical and play nasty, but they dominate because of their height and athleticism.

Eric walks over to me. Sees them in action.

"They will be tough if we play them," he says.

As he says this, one of the guys lobs a pass, and Henry catches it and dunks.

Jeez.

We grab lunch at a burger spot, a custom turkey burger and garlic-and-Parmesan fries.

I need a nap, but we have one more game to go. If we win, tomorrow we play in the final.

When we return to the court, I notice it's packed with more people. The previous games had a few spectators, but the crowds were spread out with so many games.

The group around us is filled with celebrities and athletes. I even notice a former Laker player hanging out.

"Dude, that's Marquis's son," points out Eric.

I look and see Dre Jackson. He's Marquis Jackson's son, the great former Laker who played with Magic, but his son is the real deal at age fourteen. The kid is already six foot two and puts out insane highlight tapes. His crew is his school teammates. These guys are good. We might be in over our heads.

Trina, Eric, and I look at each other.

"This might be our toughest game," she admits.

It also doesn't help when Dre has his own fan base. We're playing to their home-court advantage. We only have Trina's parents and Allie. Eric said his parents couldn't make it today.

A celebrity basketball game just wrapped, and more people are coming to our game now that that one has concluded.

They move us to a more central court right under the ESPN sign.

Feels surreal. The pressure builds.

Dre's team is called the Jelly Rolls, and their uniforms are sicker than ours. They look metallic like shields. I'm not telling Trina that, though.

I mean, she named our team after me.

We take our practice drills and warm-ups. The ref blows the whistle.

Eric takes a deep breath. In terms of height, he's our five, and Trina and I, if you can say, are playing the three and point.

The Rolls get the rock first. Dre is a proper slash and drive player, and he's fast. He quickly bolts to the lane and goes up for an easy layup until I see Trina slap the ball from his hands right off his leg. Our ball.

He looks stunned, and so does the crowd.

I can see his eyes go large.

The ref tosses the ball to me to inbound. Trina zigzags and cuts around Eric's pick to the free-throw line where I chest pass it. She grabs it and fires. Nothing but net.

The crowd roars. And Trina starts to develop a cult following.

Dre tries to keep up with Trina, but she puts on a clinic. I don't think any of us had anticipated her ferocity. Bey with the ball. She scores in every way possible, even though they try double-teaming her. She is on a faster bit rate than others.

I'm there observing, I feel. Eric and I create room, and once in a while, when she hits traffic, she dishes to us, and we have an accessible bank off the glass or finger roll.

Dre starts his own show against us. We try switching defense on him, but he aggressively attacks the basket and keeps the game close. He turns on the jets and pulls up for a two.

We fall behind: 13–12. This time our double team pressures them to turn the ball over. Trina takes advantage and hits a long two-point shot that would make Steph blush.

We're up 14–13 now. All we need is another basket. The crowd is going crazy. Dre crouches down ninja-style and pulls on his shorts as he faces Trina. She's at least a foot shorter, but he's not taking any chances.

I pop out on the wing and catch her pass. She signals she wants the ball back. I'm not messing with her in this manner. This is her game. I return it to her.

She steps back for an iso with Dre. He smirks back at her. She maneuvers into a triple-threat position. She jabs, steps toward the baseline, and drives. She pump-fakes and gets Dre in the air. He looks like he's going to swat the shot. She pivots and pirouettes toward the basket in slow motion instead of shooting. One of the other defenders rises to block her shot, but she hesitates, and he flies by, and finger rolls it off the glass. The ball hits the perfect angle and goes in. I leap up in excitement. However, I notice Trina land and crumble to the ground holding her knee.

She winces. It's the same knee she hurt at the wedding. Eric and I quickly run toward her, as do Uncle and Kaki. Trina clutches her knee. I can see her grit her teeth. She never shows pain, but I can now see her almost in tears.

A few seconds later, an emergency doctor comes in and examines her.

All the other crowds surround us.

I overhear Dre say, "That girl can ball," to his squad.

After a few minutes, Trina leans up. The doctor tries bending her knee. She clenches her fist in anger.

"I'll be fine," she says.

Kaki asks the doctor if she tore it.

"I don't know," he says. "We have to get it examined."

"No way, I'm fine," Trina insists. "It's just bruised. Kobe tore his Achilles and still hit a free throw."

She tries to get up, but she can't. Eric and I help her to her feet to carry her away, her arms around our shoulders.

As we walk past the rest of the spectators, Dre and his teammates give Trina a dap and tell her she's a legend. The crowd applauds.

Trina's in pain, but she manages to grind out a smile.

I've never seen someone do what she did.

She asks me who we are playing next. I'm told it's going to be Henry's team, The Hotsteppers. But with only two people, we might be disqualified.

When we get home, Trina doesn't want to hear any of it. Uncle and Kaki tell her it's over. She tosses the ice bag in their direction.

I'm okay with us being done. We got this far. But Trina limps toward me and tells me we are going to win.

"Pain is the little voice in your head," she says to me, quoting, as always, Kobe.

I don't sleep much of the night. I check on Trina, and her leg is elevated and iced. It's swollen.

She hears me leaving the room, probably because Bean makes so much noise.

"Tomorrow is your time, bro," she says, the lamp glowing in the dark.

"But how? We can't win without you," I say, completely dejected.

"I'll be there, but it's your time to shine," she says, squeezing my shoulder.

The following day Trina is up. She's limping, but she wears her brace and extra padding. Uncle and Kaki plead with her to rest, but she won't hear it.

They give in after she agrees she'll get the knee examined after the game.

Eric is also shocked that she wants to play.

I'm not sure why she's taking the chance. But she's Trina, and that's what she does.

We check in at the registration area when we return to LA Live. The judges look at Trina's limping and ask if she can play. She insists she can.

Henry bumps into us. He and his crew have dyed their hair blond.

He looks at Trina, Eric, and me.

"Raam, I got a message from a friend of yours. We are pals on IG."

He shows me his phone.

There's a video from Payton.

"Yo, Raam, don't get posterized again," Payton says, laughing at the camera.

The video ends.

Seeing his face again and remembering the horror of that time takes over my mind and part of me wants to run away.

Trina swats the phone away, and she moves me in the opposite direction.

"Don't worry about his cheap tactics," she says. "He's trying to get in your head."

Henry laughs, walks away, and blows a fake kiss to Allie. I keep staring in a daze.

Trina shakes me. She stares right into my face.

"Listen, you need to be a lion," she demands. "A lion seeks food, whatever he's gonna kill and eat. And you know how many bugs are on the lion's eyes and gnats on his body? He's so locked in on that zebra that he doesn't get distracted by anything else. You're not as locked in if you get distracted by little things. Be a lion."

"You stole that from Kobe."

"Bruv, be a lion," she repeats.

Henry and his teammates would be a tough battle even at full strength. With Trina limited in her movement, our obstacle is uphill.

And now, Payton's in my head, and I can't forget what happened. Aron's face turned away in shame.

I take a deep breath and try to think of the lion.

"Don't forget all you learned," Trina says.

I know the focus will be on Eric, but we have to give the impression that Trina is at full strength or that she can play.

We get the ball first. I bounce a pass to Trina. She takes a quick jumper, and it goes in. Her movement is stilted, but she's gnashing through.

At least now, they have to give her some attention.

Our game plan is to create enough plays for Eric in the paint and use me as the outside threat. The hard part is defense. We have to play like it's two-on-one, like a shorthanded hockey team.

And we can't play zone, either.

For a while, we put up a solid fight. We're only down 7–5. When Henry showboats his dribbling skills and takes me down the lane, he leaps over me as Payton did, but I stand and take charge this time. The ref blows the whistle.

He dunks it, but it doesn't count.

They double-team Eric now, and I realize it's my show. I go back to the days of playing at the courts at Storybrook West, where it was me and Cake shooting.

Also, I remember I have a left hand that was always my weakness. Now it's not.

I have Henry isolated, and I fake going right and going left. This gives me plenty of space, and I shoot a three. I drain it.

We go back and forth, and Henry and his team have a 14–13 lead. We get the ball back on a missed jumper. I dish it to Trina, and she gives it back to me. I have a wide-open three, and I know I can win the game if I take it, but Henry is in my face.

If this was the beginning of summer, I would have taken the shot. But after all that's gone down, all the mental anguish, embarrassment, and loss. This is my moment. This is what all these lessons are for. I can feel the flow that I remembered from the dock. The ease of playing. Not forcing the issue. Let the fish come to me. I feel light, calm, serene, and peaceful even with Henry steamrolling me.

I'm not making the same mistake twice, and I fake like I'm going to jack it up, but instead, Eric cuts to the basket. It's like slow motion, frame by frame. I dish it off to him. He dunks it. Game tied.

"Nice pass, Raam," Eric says, giving me a fist pound.

And now, it's our ball.

I check it for Henry and pass it to Trina. She gets swarmed and tosses it back to me. I try to toss it to Eric, but he cuts the other direction, and I throw the ball out of bounds.

I point at myself.

"My bad, y'all," I say. "That's my fault."

Trina and Eric walk over to me, and we briefly huddle.

"We have to stick to them like glue," Trina says, favoring the knee.

Henry takes the ball from the sideline and dishes it to his teammate. Trina tries to cover, but the guy beats her off the dribble and quickly dishes to Henry. Henry's wide open, but I sneak behind him and punch the ball away toward Trina. Eric grabs it and tosses it back to me. I spy Trina wide open in the corner. I also have a chance to shoot it, but I throw a bounce pass that splits the defense toward Trina. She retrieves it and fires a three from the baseline.

The ball arcs over and swishes in the net.

Eric and I swarm toward Trina, euphoric, elated.

There's no better feeling that fills me as we hug one another.

"Incredible shot," I say to Trina.

"Dude, that pass was unbelievable," she says to me. "Raam,

that was a heads-up play. You were a lion out there."

Henry looks stunned on the sidelines, a towel covering his face.

I can see phones taking photos.

The judges come out to us with the trophy. Eric, Trina, and I hoist it in the air. We are the champions, my friends.

On the speakers, I hear: "Congratulations to the Raamstars for winning the Ballerfest 11–14 group! What a performance."

Trina's and Eric's parents come to greet us. Allie greets me with an extra big hug. All of us are stunned. We celebrate by eating tacos. We found Aunt Chiladas. They had set up a truck at the event. Eric is delighted.

The tacos are amazing.

We sit on a bench. Trina's leg is heavily wrapped and iced. She gave everything, and I'm hoping her leg is okay. Allie and I sit next to each other. She holds my hand, and I inhale her vanilla peach perfume.

And when we get home, she hugs me. I'm blushing.

Later that night, my phone pings:

MOM: **So proud of you. Congrats on the win.**

DAD: **Nice job, kiddo. Can't wait to see the trophy!**

I'm leaving tomorrow.

I'm folding clothes when Trina comes in. Her knee is better. The MRI confirmed it was a hyperextension. She will have to rest for a few weeks.

Bean comes and sits next to me, putting his head on my leg.

As I'm packing my bag, I come across the Raamstar shirt she made for us, and an idea sparks in my mind.

"What do you think about starting a clothing brand called Raamstar?"

Her eyes light up. "When life gives you lemonade, you make your own T-shirt. Like Kobe, you can reinvent yourself. You can manipulate an opponent's strength and use it against them."

"What do you mean?"

"Make the clothing company about your experience and make it a statement for overcoming something. Like those people who go viral and copyright their memes to make money."

Trina is a smart cat.

"This is brilliant."

"You know, Eric's dad is the perfect person to talk to."

"Really?" I ask.

"Yeah, that's what he does. I remember him helping Marley Bit My Toe kids monetize their video. When he comes by, I'll talk to him. But listen, I got something for you."

Trina gives me a wrapped gift in a yellow-and-purple bow.

"What is it?" I ask.

"Open it."

I slice open the wrapping paper and find a book.

It's *The Alchemist* by Paulo Coelho.

"It was Kobe's favorite book and it's one of mine."

"Thanks!"

"It's my summer reading assignment for you."

"You have no idea how much you taught me."

"Bro, that's what older sisters are for," she says, smiling. "That and kicking your butt in ball."

She gives me a big hug.

Eric and Allie come by before I leave.

Eric tells me his dad is excited to talk to me and will give me a call in a few days.

He also shows me his new pair of XJs. He found a pair from another dealer.

Allie hugs me and gives me a peck on the cheek. She tells me her show is debuting in two weeks, and she gives me her number and tells me to text her when I get back home.

Uncle, Kaki, and Trina drop me off at the airport. LAX still feels vast. The weather is perfect, and I'm hesitant to leave.

"I left some of that mix for you," Uncle says. "Remember good hygiene."

Kaki says she put in some bhusu mix as well. They both burst out laughing.

"Don't worry about your parents," Kaki says. "Everything will work out."

Her face looks like it's got full movement back.

Trina punches me playfully in the shoulder.

"Remember, iron sharpens iron, little bro."

Outside, the sun is setting over the mountains, perfectly themed with purple and gold colors.

I close my eyes and absorb it all one last time. And then I head in. I have a goal to make the team this year, and nothing will stop me. It's not going to be easy. No one will outwork me.

HOME IS WHERE THE HOOP IS

I take the late-night flight back home. Now I know why they call it the red-eye.

I can't sleep on the plane. My mind keeps playing over the events of the last month and how things have changed. California felt like home.

I would like to know if things will be the same when I get to Florida: if Mom and Dad can live in the same house, if Cake and I can be friends again, and if I have really moved on from the Payton incident.

These worries tug me underwater in my head. Still, I remember I had to maintain my Mamba mentality, as Trina taught me.

I pull *The Alchemist* out of my bag, turn the pages, and find a quote that puts me at ease.

"The secret of life, though, is to fall seven times and to get up eight times."

I was free-falling, but now I won't back down.

Nothing says welcome back to Florida more than stepping through the automatic double doors out of the frigid airport into the deep, humid sauna of the arrivals area.

Mom and Dad pick me up.

I'm surprised. They look less tired and stressed. Dare I even say happier?

"You look like you've tanned nicely," Mom says, her eyes a green sea of calm and serenity. "And you've grown taller."

"Something about that California sun and dry air," I remark.

She squeezes me tightly. I notice her hair is dyed pink and purple.

She catches my stare.

"Thought I'd go punk."

"I dig it," I tell her.

"How was your trip?" Dad asks. His face looks refreshed, like he spent time at a resort spa. He hugs me.

"Any earthquakes?" he asks. His hair is trim, and he looks like he lost weight.

I remember that day I forgot even to tell them about my first one.

"Yeah, it was a 4.5," I tell them. "It knocked down some books and DVDs."

He laughs.

"Told you," he says.

"You're right," I admit. "I'd rather deal with hurricanes."

"Weren't you in the bathroom when we experienced our first?" Mom says, laughing at Dad.

Dad starts cracking up too.

We buckle our belts. I notice Mom holding Dad's hand as we drive. Both their wedding rings are on. I fall back in the seat and take a deep breath.

Dad notices me looking.

"Raam, we started counseling," Dad says.

"Oh, that's good," I say. "How's it going?"

"Well, we are working through it," Mom says.

"That's great," I say. It's all I can muster. I'm relieved and hopeful.

When we drive into the neighborhood, something is different. The jungle of grass on the course has been mowed, and the drawbridge over the pond has been fixed. I even see giant hills of sand that will be used for the bunkers.

"Are they opening up the course?" I ask Dad.

"Yeah, finally. They sold it to another company and have already begun repairing the course. I might finally be able to use my clubs."

We pull into the driveway, and I notice the front yard has new landscaping and a big new tree that looks like one I know.

"Is that a mango tree?"

"Yup, just like Bha and Dada have. We decided to grow our own mangoes."

"When are they coming back?" I ask.

"Next week."

Inside, the house feels spruced up and brighter. I put my bags down.

There's a bunch of new film equipment in the living room.

"What's all this?" I ask Dad.

I see him glance over to Mom.

"Well," she says. "Your dad left Vipul Uncle's company."

Dad wears a proud smile on his face.

"I decided it was time. Better now than never. Your mom and I talked about it. I've started my own agency."

"That's great."

I'm excited for him. And Mom's expression shows it too.

"And I'm his first client," Mom says. "He's going to shoot my new marketing video. I even have a new routine."

Mom smiles. She asks me to talk to her in the kitchen.

While Dad's adjusting one of his tripods, Mom gives me a box.

"Give it to your dad. It's a gift from both of us."

I offer the box to Dad. I have no idea what it is. He looks at me, tilting his head.

"A gift from your son," Mom says.

She winks at me.

Dad opens it, and inside is a new camera lens.

He is almost in tears and hugs us both.

"He used his card money," Mom says.

She couldn't have put the five hundred dollars to better use.

"So, that means you're going to make another movie?" I ask.

"I'm open to the idea," Mom says.

Dad looks at her, shocked.

"Really?"

"Let's take one project at a time," Mom says calmly.

I head over to my room. It hasn't changed. The posters all hang there. I grab my miniature basketball and take a few jumpers and a fadeaway, falling into my bed. Grabbing my phone, I start up Twitter. I haven't looked at it in a few days, but my mentions have a bunch of notices.

I scroll and see Aron's feed. He retweeted the last play from the Ballerfest Final. The one of me stealing the ball and making the pass.

He tagged me and wrote:

That's how you play the game, @raamstaar.
Can't wait to see what you do next.

It's been retweeted a thousand times, and the comments are positive.

It doesn't feel real. I end up crashing from sheer exhaustion.

A loud ping wakes me. It's 4 a.m. It's a message from Trina.

TRINA: **You have to work hard in the dark to shine in the light.** ☺

I text back.

ME: **I'm up.**

Five minutes later, I fall back asleep.

Later in the morning, I get up and head to the kitchen. Mom and Dad tell me they're leaving for the dance studio to do some scouting.

I grab my basketball and decide to take a stroll.

The weather is muggy and tropical, but things are different as I bounce the ball along the path. Each dribble feels soothing, like the tick of a clock. The sidewalks have been pressure washed, and sprinklers spray geysers of water on the new sod.

People are watering their plants, and I can see kids on swings and slides.

I close my eyes and pretend I'm hitting the shot in the middle school finals. There are still a few days before school starts.

I continue to walk along a path that runs adjacent to another pond. That's when I spot the duck family I noticed at the lake earlier in the summer. When I left, they were learning how to fly. Now they are bigger. As I watch them from the shore, a younger duck takes off into flight and soars in the sky, flapping its wings and quacking happily.

I can't help but smile. I feel that flow in my mind. Easy.

Finally, I head to the porch back home to sit on the swing.

As I walk back to the house, I look up and see Cake. He still looks like one of those sandhill cranes is about to attack him.

We both nod our heads at each other. I don't know what to say to him. He's grown taller. So have I.

"How was your summer?" he asks. He looks at the ground.

"It was epic," I say.

"Heard you went to LA," he says. "That's amazing."

"Yeah."

"Saw Aron retweeted you. Pretty awesome," he says, grinning.

"That was cool, I admit. Better than getting laughed at. How was Y-Ball?"

"It was okay. Wasn't the same this year."

He pauses. He bites the inside of his mouth.

"Look, bro, I'm sorry the way things went down," he says. "This was supposed to be a joint operation, not a solo venture."

I didn't see that coming. That means a lot, and I also need to admit my mistake.

"It's my fault as well. I had a lot of issues, and I'm working on them."

"It's all good."

We both nod, not knowing what to say.

"I learned a few new moves."

"We gotta capture those. My channel is starting to blow up. I actually passed Court Kings in followers."

"Noyce. You ready for tryouts?" I ask.

"Yeah, man," he says. "Wanna practice?"

"Let's do it."

We roll over to the basketball court and guess who we find—the Moores.

They've grown since we last saw them. Grown taller and more obnoxious.

We approach them.

"Rematch," I say.

"Haha," they laugh. "You got some nerve. You all are still banned. Aren't you still in hiding?"

"Summer's almost over, and yeah, I'm here, so we can demolish you," I say.

They grab their bellies and laugh.

"Scrub a dub dub," Justin says. "Let's get this over and send you back to your cribs. We'll even give you ball first."

"We're gonna destroy you," I tell them.

"Yeah, gonna wipe the floor with your faces," Cake says surprisingly. I nod my head at him in approval. He returns the favor.

We exchange our patented handshake and dap.

"Spice Brothers, on one, two, three. Garam!"

I check the ball. Dustin throws it back at me. I take a deep breath. I spot Cake cutting toward the basket.

Time to cook. It's our court now.

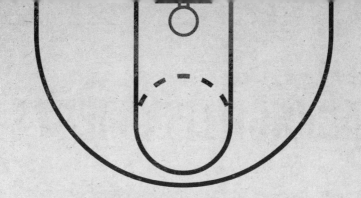

LOOK FOR PLAY THE GAME #2:
TAKE THE SHOT.
**RAAM AND CAKE TRY OUT
FOR THE MIDDLE SCHOOL
TEAM. WILL RAAM EARN A
SPOT ON THE ROSTER THIS
TIME AROUND? OR WILL
OLD RIVALS RESURFACE?**

ACKNOWLEDGMENTS

In 2020, I received an email that would change my life. Jas Perry, without your steadfast belief, support, and hustle, I'd still be riding the bench. You have been a dear friend, agent, editor, and shoulder to lean on. You are cooler than a polar bear's toenails.

Abby McAden and Anjali Bisaria, you two are the best editors a newbie like me could ask for. Thank you for making this book the best it can be. I know what Horace Grant felt like when he had Jordan and Pippen.

I still remember our chat, Matt Ringler, and it was like talking to a friend I'd known all my life. Thank you for believing in my voice and taking a chance on me. I greatly appreciate you leaving me in the hands of Abby.

This fantastic cover would only happen with the amazing artistry and design skills of Berat Pekmezci and Stephanie Yang. To my other Scholastic family: Mary Kate Garmire,

Rachel Feld, Katie Dutton, Seale Ballenger, and Lerina Velasquez, thank you.

Rajni George, thank you for helping me reach where I am today. Guissella and your two sons, Grant and Wes, for being my first readers. Rohit, for the bond that we've had since 9th grade. Julia and Christie for nudging me when I needed tough love. Kelly, thank you for always being in my corner and motivating me. Cherian, Brooke, and both Daves for trusting I could do it. Vishant for teaching me the alchemy of discipline. And friends from Diana, Tom, Kristin, Rob, and Nick. Jay and Amy Shah, Mike, Sean, John, Cam, Carmen, Mason, Mighty Oak, WLP family, Rupak, and Nancy, Rahul, Ryan, Adam, Aisha, Raaj, Tammy, Mark, Trina, and Sanjiv. TY!

Ken Lee, thank you for helping me find the right mantra.

Thank you to Tanuja Desai-Hidier, Anna John, Pooja Makhijani, Briana Peppins, Russ Bengston and Sarah Khan, Harin, Dan, Kasey, Rock, and Naresh, who always cheered me on.

To Professor William McKeen and Ms. Runyon for being amazing teachers. And a special shout-out to SAJA, MG23 group, #MGBookchat, and librarians.

And now to Chirag, Manisha, Mahendra Uncle, and Nila

Kaki. This book wouldn't be a thing without those beloved Streamwood summers that filled my childhood with warm memories. I miss you, Kaki. We all do.

To my in-laws, Mummy and Pappa, thank you for the blessing and love.

And to all my uncles, aunties, cousins, and in-laws in India and America. Thank you.

Amit, my brother, thank you for always supporting me despite my putting gum in your hair. Shelly and Raam, I appreciate all the love.

And to my lovely, sweet Tejal. Your support, belief, and sacrifice made this possible. Without your love, my words mean nothing. I love you more than you'll ever know.

For Rohan and Annika, you are the reason I wrote this. You bring me joy, inspiration, and meaning. Daddy loves you.

And to my parents, Harish and Varsha, you are the light I follow. Thank you for always setting an example for me and giving me the room to follow my dreams. Love you and JSK.

And for all those kids, remember to channel your own Mamba Mentality. Game on.